QUIET MOVE

a Charlemagne file

K.A. Bachus

Cover design by Marigold Faith

CHARLEMAGNE FILE TIMELINES

Short Story Collection
A Lighter Shade of Night,
mid 60s to early 70s

Novels
Trinity Icon, early 70s
Cetus Wedge, early 80s
Brevet Wedge, nine months later
Lion Tamer, five months later
State of Nature, early 90s
Vory, a year later
Swallow, five weeks later
Quiet Move, late 90s
Goat Rope, 1999

CONTENTS

PROLOGUE

"Why not, Skosh? We were made for each other. I know you enjoyed it as much as I did." Candace had chosen a small table for two by the window. Skosh found it uncomfortably public.

"Of course I enjoyed it," he said. "I've never not enjoyed sex. That doesn't mean we're even compatible, let alone made for each other. Believe me, I would never make you happy."

He was being careful. What he meant was that she could never make him happy. She could make him horny in a manufactured scenario, but that did not equate to happiness.

A waitress appeared. Candace ordered a chef's salad and white wine. Skosh asked for coffee, black, and kept his face turned away from the window.

"This lunch is on me, Skosh. Surely you don't maintain that beautiful body of yours with just coffee?"

She blinked slowly, accentuating her large grey eyes, her finest feature. Her only fine feature thought Skosh.

She continued, "It's too early in our relationship to assume we're incompatible."

"There is no relationship, Candace."

Coffee and wine arrived. Candace sipped with a show of daintiness. Skosh gulped.

"But we should get to know each other," insisted his reptilian lunch companion. "All I know about you is that I enjoyed the other night. It made me want to know every part of you. For example, I see the contracts you work on, because that's my job, but the language is so specialized, the words don't even tell me what you do. I want to know more. Tell me."

She may as well have described an excruciating torture. As a natural spook of the old school, Skosh had so compartmentalized his life that any personal disclosure felt like a threat. But she was much more highly placed in their organization, albeit in an administrative role, and could conceivably damage him badly. He chose his next words with utmost caution.

"Candace, this is not a good idea for either of us but especially for you. Gossip can be vicious. You have a brilliant career and should not spoil it on the likes of me."

"With all due respect, Skosh, as the senior person in this relationship, that is for me to decide."

"Again. There. Is. No. Relationship."

He could not stop the vehemence with which he punctuated each word.

"But I promise you, Skosh, there will be."

Her words were sweet and smooth, like the wine she sipped, but Skosh had seen the flash of anger in those grey eyes and became as alert to danger as the hot, acidic bean brew he was drinking could make him.

ONE

Sekmet stretched a tawny foreleg, claws extended, and pulled the blanket from Penny's bare shoulder, but neither cold air nor loud purring woke her. The cat, offended by the sudden blare of the telephone, jumped away before trying again. Penny groped for the handset, knocked it off the receiver, felt around the floor by the nightstand, and picked it up by its cord.

"Hello," she croaked into the earpiece. She turned over the handset and heard a voice.

"Is this Penelope Prendergast?"

Penny squinted one eye at the alarm clock. Seven minutes past midnight.

"Who is this?" she demanded.

She recognized the name he gave as belonging to one of the muckety-mucks in Personnel.

"Ms. Prendergast," he said, "would you be willing to assist an ops guy? Your role will be strictly administrative, no danger involved."

Penny said yes, hoping secretly for at least a little bit of danger.

She fielded the usual questions. When was her last bring-up investigation? Her last polygraph? Evidently, her answers satisfied him. She hoped asking a question of her own would not irritate.

"When?"

"Now. Pack a bag. Leave all identification at home. He'll pick you up in front of your apartment in fifteen minutes."

Only after the call ended did she think it might have been nice to know who was picking her up and kicked herself for missing the opportunity to ask. Ready in five minutes, including makeup and the unsnarling of a nest of dark hair, she made her way downstairs and outside in seven, then stood waiting, freezing, for twenty. It dawned on her as she shivered that she had packed only winter clothes. What if the op was in a warm climate? Maybe someplace tropical? Another question she forgot to ask—where?

She debated running upstairs for lighter clothes until a black government sedan pulled up at the main entrance. The driver climbed out, took her bag, and opened a back door for her. He put her suitcase in the trunk as she sat on the back seat. There were no interior lights. The man next to her could have been anybody. Well, he is in black ops, she told herself. What do you expect? Of course, they take this shit seriously.

"I've cleared you for WEDGE material," he said. He had a smooth baritone voice, but she could not see his face or gauge his size in the dark car, though she felt his bulk.

"There is no file by that name in my document vault," she said.

"There fucking better not be."

This was a marked departure from other polished executives she met in this job, solemn visitors in business suits who signed into the large inner vault where the most sensitive documents in her library sheltered behind thick concrete and steel.

This man reminded her more of people she had knew in the Army, both men and women, accustomed to the talented use of the language of stress. She found it refreshingly real and disturbingly aggressive in this civilian context.

Occasional streetlights revealed no more about her companion aside from a head of dark hair. Unrelenting dark shadowed his face. After a long, silent interval, he said, "I'll brief you on the airplane."

She screwed up her courage. "This is not the way to either airport."

"Correct. They've sent one of theirs."

She had no idea who 'they' were nor what of theirs they might send. Nobody could send a third airport, could they? So far, the dots in this sparse conversation did not connect. They didn't even suggest a pattern. Just a random spattering, like paint flung off a brush.

They drove through a wooded area and onto the taxiway of a dark airfield she never knew existed. The car stopped next to a black Lear 45. In the headlights, a red-haired woman opened the cargo compartment. Jade's shadowy new boss did not introduce them as he grabbed their bags from the trunk and threw them into the cargo compartment. Jade stood cold and awkward to one side.

"How's it going, Claire?" he asked the woman.

"Good. I'm still loving the job."

"Are you in command this trip?"

"I am."

"I feel safer just knowing that."

He took Penny's arm and guided her to the stairs, steadying her from behind as she climbed into the gloomy cabin. Small, dim floor lights kept her from walking into black shapes of low tables and large seats. The window shades were fastened down; she could see no hint of the lighter shade of starlight outside. The man helped her into an overstuffed armchair of a seat, found one end of her seat belt, and dug under her hip for the other, oblivious to her gasp. She still could not see his face but caught a whiff of expensive aftershave.

As the wheels came up after takeoff, the cabin lights came on and she saw her traveling companion for the first time. He faced her across a small table. The first thing she noticed was the way his shirt stretched across wide shoulders supporting a holster bearing a semi-auto. He was tall—she estimated six feet and a little—and Asian, with black hair, black eyes, and a well-formed jaw. She thought he might be approaching forty.

He did not wear a wedding ring, something she checked as a habit, especially when she met a man as appealing as this. It heartened her until she remembered that as a black ops operative, he was not likely to wear a ring. She probably wouldn't even be told his real name.

"Call me John Nakamura," he said. "It's my game name. Everybody calls me Skosh. Penelope Prendergast? Really?"

"My mother is a hopeless romantic. Please call me Penny."

"No. Normally an admin-type shouldn't need a game name, but with these guys, it's not advisable to use your real name. Especially not one as distinctive as yours. It won't take them long to find you either way, but it's not good policy to make it too easy."

He pulled a sealed envelope out of the coat draped over the back of his seat and handed it to her.

"Your name for this op is Jade Wilmerton. Personnel made up your shoes. I did not ask them to generate a legend for you because there was no time. If you are unlucky enough to come into contact with the team, you can give the unclassified part of your job description, nothing more. Stay away from personal details. I will do my best to keep you out of that situation, but shit happens. Be prepared."

He might as well have been speaking a foreign language for all she understood of it and as if to read her mind, he brought that up.

"You speak any languages?"

"French. I attended the Sorbonne for a couple of years." She did not mention her computer languages, because they were not spoken, except to a machine.

"German? Russian?"

She shook her head. He sighed. It seemed she was already a disappointment to this beautiful man.

She opened the envelope containing her operational shoes and found a passport, driver's license, and credit card in the name of Jade Wilmerton. Both passport and license included recent pictures, neither of them flattering. You can take realism too far, she thought. The passport had a few French, British, and Canadian entry stamps. They knew where she had been, though the dates were slightly off.

"Officially, you're coming along to manage the landlord, the food, and the cars and make sure everybody gets paid." He paused to drink from a water bottle. "You should drink water. Flying is dehydrating. There's a refrigerator in the back. Help yourself."

When she returned with a bottle of water, he resumed his briefing in a low voice.

"You'll do those admin-type things, of course, but there is another reason I'm bringing you with me and we will get to that when we land and find a secure place to talk. For now, understand that I intend to keep you as far as possible from the team. Please cooperate with me on that."

This was a second reference to a team. She raised her eyebrows and tilted her head forward.

"Don't ask," he said.

That made her even more curious.

He spoke again before she could get the question out. "And don't go around trying to find out. I will tell you what you need to know, like the fact that they are dangerous. There, I just told you everything you need. Don't be curious. Don't think about what I'm doing. Just do the job I ask you to do."

"Yes, Sir."

"And cut the military shit. I hear enough of it from Claire up front. Even though she's the boss when we fly, she sirs me all the time. Incidentally, be careful when you talk to her. She works for them, not us."

Penny drew up some courage and asked, "Where are we going?"

She hoped for a smidgeon of information that at least would tell her if the bag she brought would turn out to be useless for the climate.

"Lithuania, on the Baltic coast. I hope you packed warm clothes. It's more than a bit of a hike to get there, so I recommend you get as much sleep as you can now."

This was welcome news. So was his assistance with her seat. It had to be the most comfortable airplane seat ever made. Once he configured hers for sleep, he adjusted his own and doused the overhead lights. He did not snore. Penny hoped with all her heart that she did not. She woke twice, once when they touched down in Goose Bay and then in Reykjavik, but she didn't try to raise the shade next to her seat. Too tired to wonder about these places for long, she fell asleep again.

She woke fully the third time the airplane touched down and rehearsed her new name internally to make it her own. She sensed a different quality in the activity around her. Skosh stood and donned his coat in the dark cabin. Penny had considerable difficulty getting out of her seat because she didn't know which button did what. He simply took her hand and pulled her up, then handed over her coat.

The airplane taxied along the ramp in a place she never heard of called Palanga. Skosh was about to say more when Claire stepped into the cabin.

"I think it's only fair to tell you the Challenger is here."

"Fuck! They're two days early." Skosh paused, then said through his teeth, "You told them I brought someone, didn't you?"

"I know who I work for, Skosh. Don't tell me you're surprised."

"She's just an administrative assistant."

"I'm not the one you'll need to convince."

Penny could feel Skosh fuming beside her. He took quick, hissing breaths and loosened the fists his hands had been making. She tried to lighten the tension by using her friendliest voice, pretending the man next to her, her new boss, was not about to explode for reasons beyond her understanding.

"Hi," she said to the pilot, "My name is Jade Wilmerton."

"Call me Claire." Turning to Skosh, Claire continued, "You and Jade are requested to board the

Challenger the minute you deplane. It will be in the next parking spot. Please try to remember your manners, Skosh, and use something other than your usual string of f-words when you introduce Jade to Charlemagne."

TWO

"Don't say anything. Let me do the talking," Skosh murmured as they crossed the tarmac to the Challenger parked next to them.

Jade was smiling too much. He doubted anything he said had gotten through to her. Her palpable excitement made her step bouncy, swinging her glossy, deep auburn hair around her shoulders. It increased his sense of doom. This fiasco might kill him.

The roomy main cabin of the Challenger had been updated since the last time he was inside, several years before. They stepped into what could be mistaken for a stylish living room, with eight overstuffed chairs arranged in two shallow semicircles. Clear space in the center would accommodate a conference table, probably something that dropped from the ceiling or rose from the floor, Bond-style, but presently absent. The team occupied five seats as comfortable as those in the Lear.

Charlie, son of the team's leader, Mack, nodded to Jade and pointed at the seat between him and his father. With a minimal lift of his chin, he banished Skosh to the other side of the cabin, isolating Jade between the two blue-eyed men who ran the team.

"What languages do you speak?" asked Mack, when Jade had settled into the seat next to him.

Skosh answered for her. "She speaks French."

There came a long silence as Mack stared at him. He stared back, doing his best to scrub out any hint of belligerence.

"Good," said Mack, "we will use French."

"Except that I don't have any French," protested Skosh.

"I expect you will remedy that deficiency soon."

Skosh nodded slightly.

The cabin harbored the usual suspicious undercurrents, now augmented by the presence of a non-operational woman who was too attractive for her own good. And Skosh was the guilty party who had introduced her. Let's see, he thought, how many complications have I created? As if we needed more. He probed the air around him and the breath within. Tension certainly, perhaps a touch more than usual, followed by way more suspicion, and... there it was—he could almost taste it in the air around him—latent violence.

He felt it in every word, every glance, every subtle effort to loosen tensed muscles. It was their default reaction to mistakes like this. He had introduced an unknown element on an operation already nudging the outer limits of possibility. The team known as Charlemagne didn't become the best in the business—they didn't stay alive, in other words—by making allowances.

He could see Mack was not happy as he turned again to Jade, subjecting her to his most quelling glare. Her brown eyes became saucers. Skosh knew the innocence in that expression would not protect her. It might even do the opposite. It would deepen suspicion.

"Skosh calls me Mack and the game name of the man to your left is Charlie," he said. "The others will introduce themselves in time. What may we call you?"

"Jade," said Skosh, again rushing to answer. "Jade Wilmerton."

Another long silence, then a feminine voice across the cabin to Skosh's right said, "It is nice to meet you, Jade. Please, call me Mara."

More strikingly beautiful than ever, thought Skosh, cutting his admiration short before Mara's husband, Sergei, should notice it. Sergei had the lethal skills to back up his jealous nature.

Jade opened her mouth to respond, probably with something polite, but the less said the better, so Skosh interrupted and changed the subject, addressing Charlie.

"You're early. I haven't had a chance to set up your safehouse yet."

"But you brought help with you," Charlie said smoothly. "It should not be difficult to move up the date." He gave Jade a pointed look. "Many people here speak German. Klaipeda, the port city nearby, was once Prussian, I understand. There is a minority who speak Polish, and most people understand Russian from the more recent Soviet times." His gaze returned to Skosh. "You have been working on that language at least, haven't you?"

"You know damn well I speak Russian now."

"I find it intriguing that you brought an administrative assistant at all. You have, before now, been sufficiently competent on your own, especially in your choice of caterers."

The others nodded their agreement.

"Turner is better at coffee," said Steve Donovan. He sat next to Sergei, his fellow delinquent, as Skosh liked to call them.

"Did you bring Jade to make coffee?" Charlie asked.

Skosh glowered in reply.

"Perhaps," said Sergei, enjoying an attempt at mischief, "she is his lover." His light grey eyes examined her more thoroughly than was strictly polite. Mara frowned at him.

"I see from Jade's reaction that this also is not the case," said Mack. "Keep your temper, Skosh. Now tell me, Miss Wilmerton, what are you allowed to reveal about your occupation? We know you did not come to make coffee, though you will do that also. What are your usual duties?"

Skosh could give her no help and instead made his face a blank study in unconcern, hoping she would remember his earlier advice.

"I'm a librarian."

"Ah, then your business is information. Skosh has brought a librarian who speaks none of the most prevalent languages of this country to help him with his already more than competent catering, and he wonders why we question this." Mack turned to Skosh. "You must see your plan to shield her from us has failed. I have canceled Miss Wilmerton's hotel reservation. She must stay with you in your safehouse. You know you cannot protect her from us. It remains to be seen whether we can protect her from our enemies or whether we will want to."

"You canceled it? How did you even know about it?" Forcing his words through clenched teeth strangled them.

Mack's answer came in the form of a gaze with slow blinks and a minimal head tilt, the kind of telepathic communication Skosh had learned to interpret. Danger is not imminent, it said but can escalate quickly, depending on your behavior. I will know why you did this in a short while and you will know my decision the moment I make it.

The blue stare helped Skosh find the inner resources needed to control his temper. He relaxed his jaw, looked away, and said, "I see. My assistant will have you in the safehouse in four hours. Come along, Jade."

"I think she should stay with us while you make arrangements," said Charlie.

"Stop winding up the babysitter, Charlie," said Steve in a slow drawl. "He has finally found us two safehouses so we don't have to look at his ugly mug all the time."

"But I want very much to look at his assistant," replied Charlie, still using that soft, smooth voice. "As much as possible."

He looked her in the eye as he said this, but only briefly because Skosh was hauling her through the door, catching her as she fell down the first three steps.

"That man is scary," she said when she regained her feet.

He let her go when he was sure she was steady and looked at her again through a different lens. Could she be his type? Who was he fooling? Any reasonably attractive woman with a pulse was his type. That wasn't why he looked again. Her reaction to Charlie suggested there might be more to her than wearing a Burberry coat to a black op might suggest.

She smiled up at him under a waxing moon, full of trust and questions.

If she is no more than fluff, he thought, what I have done to her is inexcusable. If she is more than that, it's also intolerable. Great. Now I have sunk so low as to measure her damage by its effect on me. He set his jaw and looked away before responding.

"Yeah. Stay clear of Charlie. We have a shit-ton of things to do. The answer to Mack's question about how you were going to cope without the language is named Rimantas. We need to find him, and you'll have to glue yourself to him when you talk to the landlord. He'll translate. I think he's trustworthy. Well, maybe."

THREE

With several hours of forced inactivity ahead of them, Mara, Sergei, and Steve hoarded sleep, knowing operational needs would soon eliminate the possibility. Sergei's badly set broken nose made him snore. The Challenger jet sat reasonably secure on the ramp, with little winter traffic at the airfield and good visibility all around. Michael and his father Misha took the first watch,

Michael handed his father a mug of black coffee from the galley and sat in the seat facing him.

"You've been elevating that leg often lately, Papa. Is it worse?"

Misha winced as he shifted his left leg to ease a cramp.

"No worse than usual."

"Has Alex ...?" Michael stopped at a glare from his father.

"Has your stepmother nagged me to listen to the doctors?" said Misha. "Yes. Has she suggested I quit? No."

"I remember the argument you two had after Vasily died." Michael's mind could still hear the screaming and door slamming between his father and Vasily's widow Alex, despite the passage of a dozen years. She was now his stepmother.

Misha closed his eyes as he drank his coffee.

"I accused her of causing Vasily to go to that meeting unarmed," he said. "She swore she never spoke to him about such things, and I did not believe her. Now, I do. She avoids any mention of my work."

"Then it is not Alex who convinced you to leave more of the responsibility to me?"

"No, my leg is persuasive enough."

"But your judgment is more vital to us than the ability to run twenty kilometers, Papa. I am amazed the Americans agreed to your demand to access their information. How did you get them to accept that clause in the contract?"

Misha shrugged, a rare enough gesture. He was seldom unsure about anything. "I requested it. I am as surprised as you are that they agreed."

"I would wager Skosh did not agree." Michael gulped the last of his coffee. "He brought this woman with him to help evade the clause. I have no idea how he plans to use her."

Misha nodded. "Very true. I cannot think of a more unlikely ploy. Does he mean to distract us with her? No. He could not have agreed with that clause. It is probable he did not know about it until it was too late to make a change. The woman's presence is the result of a hasty, maybe desperate, plan to circumvent the contract. It will fail."

Michael smiled. No matter how much his father argued with Alex and assured him he would continue with the team, he sensed his drifting thoughts of retirement. How would he cope without Misha's pinpoint understanding of others? Michael was at the height of his physical powers and had much of his father's intuitive mind, but would it ever be enough?

He took a deep breath. He would have to broach the subject.

"Papa, Steve's son Danny told me he means to join the team. But it will be several years before he is ready. My brother...."

"Max should not," interrupted Misha. "If you would produce an heir there would be no problem, but as it is, given your occupation, Max may be required to inherit."

Michael suppressed a wave of resentment at this perpetual undeserved criticism and repeated his usual answer.

"Theresa and I will keep trying for a son, Papa, but Max is determined to fight, and I see no way to prevent him once he is of age, no matter how many daughters I produce. But that is a side issue. My point is that I need you to stay active at least until Danny is ready."

Misha interrupted again.

"No, you need an older version of Danny, and you need him now. I am no replacement for a young, fit fighter. Your sister is formidable for her weight, but her power is chiefly useful only when you need finesse. You, Sergei, and Steve are in your prime. So were Louis and I when you joined us. It surprised us how much faster and more nimble you were. That is what you need. Strength and speed. You have plenty of judgment."

Michael allowed himself a brief inner jubilation at this rare compliment from his father before letting his heart sink. Misha was certainly considering retirement. For the last four years, Michael had uncomfortably borne more of the burden of responsibility. But his father's presence on each operation had not only taught him how to think and decide; it acted as a buffer, a shield around his conscience.

For Michael, his father's retirement would shift the full weight of responsibility to him. He was old enough, skilled enough, physically and mentally strong enough.

But he didn't want it.

FOUR

Skosh told Jade not to worry about the cost of moving up their tenancy of the safehouses by two days, but haggling had always been a way of life for her. She got a very good price, considering the inconvenience to the landlord, not to mention the late-evening request.

She had to admit the carte blanche Skosh gave her came as a shock. Although the contents of her vault were all related to black ops, Jade's library was considered simple overhead, not part of the secret budget of the organization. As library director, she was required to account for every line item by name. Skosh had figuratively written her a blank check to get his team off the tarmac two days early and then looked at her as if she had three heads when she did so at a reasonable price.

The two safehouses comprised a kind of duplex. More like a small two-story house that had grown a cottage on one side, like a wart, thought Jade. Skosh's side consisted of a tiny single-story one-bedroom cabin sharing a long wall with the team's larger house. Their side of the duplex had two bedrooms upstairs under a steeply pitched roof. In the cabin, a small sitting area just inside the front door contained a bench seat against the outside wall, a table, and two kitchen chairs. Both houses were heated by wood-burning stoves which, Jade suspected, she would be required to tend. Making coffee seemed like light duty in comparison.

Skosh had brought a small 240-volt coffee maker and set it up on top of an unplugged two-burner electric stove near the table. They needed the plug for the coffee maker. Jade fully concurred. The Army taught her that fresh coffee always trumps hot food.

The team had a larger, industrial-sized coffee machine tended by everybody except Mack and Charlie. Water heaters in both houses were electric, thank heaven. Skosh's had been squashed into a corner next to a tiny refrigerator. There was no heat in what was being inaccurately called 'Jade's bedroom', but the room was snug and the down duvet did its job. She just never had time to fully enjoy it.

They stood in the kitchen of their safehouse that night discussing sleeping arrangements. Skosh insisted she use the lone bedroom and directed her to buy a good lock for it. "Not that it'll do any fucking good," he muttered.

He covered catering procedures next.

"You'll take delivery of the food in here, then I will bring it next door. I'm sure Mara will help me coordinate that. As long as she's around, Sergei won't bother you. Maybe now that he's married Steve might be safe … -ish."

"I should help you bring the food," Jade suggested, "or we should have it delivered over there." She pointed at the wall they shared with the team's safehouse.

"The caterers were vetted by my Lithuanian contact," he said, "but nobody should see any of the team, and that house is not a lot bigger than this, so there are bound to be strays in and out of whatever room we try to take delivery in. It's safer for me to bring it over there."

"Then I should help you with that, Skosh. Why are you so worried?"

Jade did not allude to the as-yet unknown additional task he wanted her to do. Watching him check under and behind every picture and stick of furniture for signs of listening devices reminded her it was better not to bring up things he could not discuss openly. She had to admit she was becoming impatient to find a secure place to talk, but this certainly was not it, as noises on the other side of the wall grew louder.

He opened his mouth to answer and might have said a word, but she could not hear it because of the low explosion that sent a ribbon of plaster hurtling toward them, covering their clothes in white powder. She watched a roughly rectangular line of missing plaster appear on the wall to her left. As the air cleared, a light from the other side shone through that thin line.

"What the fuck?" Skosh shouted.

He had to shout it. Someone was noisily kicking the rectangle and it had begun to fall. A second cloud of dust settled slowly and revealed two men standing in their kitchen.

Skosh turned purple with rage.

"What the fuck do you think you're doing, Pavlenko? We have to pay for that. You are not going to have free access to this house. That was the whole point of having a second house."

The man they called Steve, the one with the southern accent, held up a hand. "Hold on there, Skosh. Sergei, tell him."

"It occurs to me you cannot carry food between the two houses without being seen and causing remarks," said Sergei. Jade recognized a

Russian accent. "I have solved problem. It is not a load-bearing wall."

"And besides, Skosh," added Steve, "with the addition of your assistant here, we're thinking the real purpose of the second house is a need for privacy. You should thank me for not letting him put a hole in the bedroom wall."

The man had begun to frankly inspect her, in detail, in an assessing manner. She would have been angry, certainly, frightened, if it did not make her tingle just a little in certain places. He had that effect, she suspected, on many women. He saw her eyes widen and gave her a knowledgeable half-smile. Skosh scowled and took a step forward.

Holding up a hand, Steve said, "Down, Fido. I won't encroach."

Her boss took a deep breath and loosened the fists he had formed.

Steve turned away and said over his shoulder, "Yet."

Jade wondered what Skosh would have done if Sergei had not stopped him before he could reach the man. The stopping was not exactly gentle, and it took the scary guy, Charlie, to put an end to it.

"The last thing I need is a babysitter unhinged by a woman, Skosh. She's yours, all yours. I will enforce it. Satisfied? Can we get on with it? You had better clean up this mess and find something to cover that hole before the caterers get here with breakfast."

Skosh took a colorful woven rug from under the woodpile beneath the kitchen table and tried to stuff it artistically into the hole. Sergei gave him a hammer and a few nails from something called the Footlocker of Useful Things and the result turned out to be quite decorative, once Jade had brushed away a few spiders displaced from their snug woodpile.

She swept debris into a dustpan as Skosh knelt, holding it in place. He looked up at her.

"After breakfast," he whispered through his teeth, "buy a very, very stout lock."

FIVE

Jade ate breakfast alone in the tiny kitchen, while Skosh sat with the team and stayed in their main room for meetings. He had handed her a penciled note on a scrap of printer paper with a list of things she should look for with Rimantas in Klaipeda. He included an unnecessary instruction to thoroughly destroy the paper.

Her interpreter arrived before she finished eating, but she was glad he interrupted what had become an empty, unwanted chewing exercise accompanied by vacant speculation.

"Call me Rimas," he said as he put an old Ško-da sedan into gear. "Where do you wish to go?"

Jade had spent several hours with him the evening before, haggling with the landlord. On this bright, cold morning she noticed how young he was, and at the same time, how old. His boyish face turned toward her, looking through blue eyes that seemed older, though he couldn't be more than thirty. He carried his tall, lanky frame with a loose-limbed, athletic gait and wore his dark-brown hair a bit on the long side. The smile arrested her immediately, mischievous but eager to please. She could not help liking him.

Knowing Skosh's ambivalence about trusting the young man, Jade spoke carefully, but she desperately wanted a friend just now and hoped Rimas would not disappoint her.

The safehouses were in a village named Juod-krantė, set back from the long primary road that served the entire length of the Curonian Spit. To the south was the Russian border at Kaliningrad. Rimas headed east and drove onto a ferry that took them across the Curonian Lagoon and into the Lithuanian port city of Klaipeda.

He led Jade down a narrow street no wider than an alley that ended near the harbor. Despite the barrier presented by forests and shifting dunes on the spit across the lagoon, wind coming off the Baltic whistled through the street as if in a tunnel.

It shook the wooden signs over shop doors and pierced her prized winter coat, a genuine Burberry she had found in a thrift shop back home. Her teeth chattered with cold as they entered a wondrous establishment dedicated to everything iron, from hinges and nails to doorknobs and locks.

The proprietor proudly set out five stout iron methods of securing a door. He and Rimas engaged in a lively, cheerful conversation. Rimas translated, holding a particularly heavy iron deadbolt.

"He says this one has been known to delay the KGB long enough to allow their quarry to escape through a window."

The man continued in Lithuanian watching her face. Rimas laughed and again translated. "Unfortunately, the window was quite high, and the man fell heavily, but neighbors dragged him away and hid him until he caught his breath and could row a boat. The KGB made sure to watch even high windows after that."

What struck her, besides the joy with which they talked about the past as being past, was the communal sense of shared truth, of common enemies and common defense.

She bought the stout lock.

They passed another cubby-hole of a shop which she could not resist browsing through. Piled high with boxes of new and husks of old computers and their parts, the shop provided a physical tour of recent cyber history. Though she was not sure how she would use it, she recognized and bought an intriguing old encryption modem card and a necessary new notebook computer. It came at an irresistible price in litas, the Lithuanian currency.

As she climbed into the car, Jade felt an attraction to her younger companion that surprised her, though it was nowhere near as compelling as what she felt when near Skosh.

"I have an older brother," Rimas said as if he read her thoughts about his age.

She smiled. "Is he as good-looking as you?"

"Better. But he is what you call in English, gay. He has invited us to lunch. Would you like to meet him?" There was a cautious quality to the question as if he expected her to say no.

"Yes, of course. How kind of him to invite me."

Antanas lived on the third floor of an ancient stone building with an elaborately tiled entrance. They climbed a broad staircase graced by carved wooden railings on either side. The aroma of good food reached Jade as their host opened the door. He was as elegant as his apartment, tall and graceful with long hair and a handsome face made more interesting by a nose with just a suggestion of beakiness. A magnificent set of drums dominated his high-ceilinged living room.

"Do your neighbors like your drums?" she asked.

He laughed and shook his head.

Antanas understood simple English but kept Rimas busy acting as a translator on more complex ideas. The three were soon laughing over a glass of pretty decent wine and Jade enjoyed the delicious soup. The dense black bread that went with it made a substantial meal all by itself.

"Do you know the musician, Tommy Taurus?" asked Rimas.

"Yes. I love his music. Why?"

"They were lovers."

"Really?" She looked at Antanas, allowing her amazement to show. Then her face fell and registered the alarm she felt for him with her next thought.

"Wait. Didn't Tommy die of AIDS?"

"Yes, but he contracted the disease after he went back to America," said Antanas. "It took him very quickly. I am unaffected, except by his loss." He became somber and refilled her glass. "I miss him badly. He gave me this flat, you know." He said something else in Lithuanian and Rimas took up the explanation.

"While I can live at home with our parents," he said, "our father does not … he will not allow …" Rimas sighed as Antanas watched for her reaction. "If Tommy had not been so generous, my brother would have no place to live. Apartments can be difficult to find."

"Tommy saved my life when he was here," said Antanas.

"He was here?"

Antanas nodded. "We met during one of his visits to his mother. She was Lithuanian. His father is American. Now that he is gone, I have only this apartment to remind me how happy we were. He told me never to let it go and he promised it would keep me safe. I will never sell it."

Safe. She had only recently been introduced to her lack of safety and here was a man acutely aware of how precarious life could be.

...

Skosh's house in Juodkrantė seemed deserted when they pulled up. Rimas helped her gather her packages and stood outside the car gazing at the house. The drawn curtains gave it an uncommonly forlorn air.

"I will wait here to be sure you have no trouble getting in," he said. "Wave to me if all is well when you open the door."

She had spent the better part of the last ten hours in the presence of armed men and watched them blow a hole in the kitchen wall for the purpose of catering, but it was her interpreter's concern for her that made her shiver.

Skosh let her in, and she waved to Rimas.

"Where the fuck have you been?"

Despite this stark contrast to a pleasant morning, Skosh managed to make her heart flutter with an almost schoolgirl crush. She kicked herself for it, but he looked tired, harried, and magnificent.

"You said to buy a lock."

"All fucking morning?"

She eyed him carefully. Coffee stained his white shirt. He had rolled up his sleeves and taken off his coat but not his weapon. His hair stuck out at wild angles, in straight, black tufts. In short, he was adorable.

After rummaging through the packages, Jade produced the prime example of ironmongery she had scored.

"See? Guaranteed to stop the KGB." She gave him her best smile.

"Did you get anything to install it with?"

Her smile fell. "I didn't think of that. Maybe Sergei's footlocker…."

"They are the people the lock is supposed to keep out."

"But if they just lend us the tools?"

She could see he wanted to make her understand. She saw him leaf through the pages of his brain searching for the perfect explanation and waited, curiously.

"What else did you buy?" he asked with a defeated sigh.

She brought out linen tea towels with sheep printed on them for the kitchen, two hand-thrown coffee mugs, an assortment of kitchen utensils, especially large wooden spoons since the food would be catered and there were never enough of those in her experience, a healthy supply of blank diskettes and finally her greatest find, the encryption card dangling on its ribbon connector.

She answered his puzzled look. "It's a…. He pushed her against the wall and clapped his hand over her mouth.

SIX

Skosh stared into her eyes, bug-eyed with the physical imposition of silence by his hand. He spoke aloud, a bit too loud, to make sure the spooks on the other side of the rug could hear him.

"Why don't we go for a walk, Jade? I could use some fresh air. How about you?" He nodded at her and slowly released his hand.

"Um. Yes, that sounds lovely. Why don't we do that?"

She matched his volume. He liked women who could catch on quickly and girls with long dark hair and … He caught himself and squashed the thought.

Grabbing his coat from a hook on the back of the door, he threw it on and pushed her out in front of him.

"Smile," he muttered. He grabbed her hand and led her down the front path to the street and across to a paved walkway along the shore.

Her hand served to warm his while he brought her half a mile away to a small deserted dry dock area with a view of Klaipeda across the lagoon. They had both left the house without gloves and her warm hand was welcome in the biting wind.

He caught himself thinking again and returned to business, taking out of his pocket the encryption modem he had grabbed from her.

"Now, tell me about this."

"It's just an interesting, somewhat old-fashioned modem for encrypting data transferring between computers. It's old, but still very effective and not easy to come by, so I bought it."

He stared at her. "You found a computer store?"

"Yes. You told me this morning you wanted me to be in a hotel with access to a computer and you gave me a note saying I should buy one. Where else would I look for one? Are you going to explain anything to me? Because as much as I think all this secret squirrel stuff is kind of sexy, not knowing what's going on does get old."

He looked in dismay at her carefully arranged hair, her designer coat, and boots and sighed. She did not belong in his world, but he wanted to belong in hers. Impossibilities sap your strength, he told himself. You're in enough fucking trouble without adding fantasies and wishes. Back to the business at hand, he made his voice gruffer than he felt.

"I told you I have another reason for bringing you. As I said this morning, I meant to put you in a hotel in Klaipeda where I could get to you, but the team couldn't. It was a forlorn hope, I know now, and you heard Mack quash it when we met on the Challenger. Even if Claire hadn't betrayed me, Mack would have known. He always knows. He reads minds."

"I have the impression Mack is not his real name."

"It's not. The others on the team call him Misha, but that name is reserved for people close to him. I don't know why; he's not Russian. My old boss named him Mack because he's famous for using a knife."

She wrinkled her brow.

He took her hand again because he needed the warmth, though he knew it was not good for him, and led her strolling along the shore, slowly.

"We're going to need reams of research and some of it will have to come from your vault. I need you to find a way to get the information I am contracted to give them. They are cleared for whatever pertains to this operation."

Skosh could see she did not understand but had the good sense to wait for him to tell her more. He wondered how much he would have to explain, and how much he could explain.

"It must be done within our established procedures, but without Mack's people knowing how you're doing it. Have you seen the new information security directive?"

Jade nodded. "Any breach, no matter how minor is guaranteed instant dismissal and maybe criminal charges." She let go of his hand and stopped. "Why not just call my office?"

He turned, took her hand again, and led her back toward the dry dock. How could he explain the professional trap that had been laid for him without whining, and more importantly, without naming names that once spoken would surely get back to Mack?

"The closest secure phone is three hours away. So I asked the personnel office for somebody who understood the system and had computer knowledge. They gave me your name. I figured only an old woman could have a name like that, so I made last-minute arrangements to bring you. I thought you'd have gray hair and sensible shoes and like I said, would stay in a hotel. Those are not sensible shoes."

He pointed at her designer half-boots with kitten heels. They went with the rest of her. Of course, she would wear kitten heels. He imagined what it would be like to work in the same office. They worked in the same building, but he wondered why he had never noticed her. Probably because she worked regular hours, with other people who also worked regular hours. He never noticed them, either.

"I got them for a very good price at a resale shop. I think they're cute. I always wanted …"

"My point is …" he interrupted, not wanting to think about kitten heels anymore. "The point is that I never intended to bring anybody, let alone a young, attractive woman, within shouting distance of those guys and here you are. I am also under a few other pressures that it's best they do not know about. They're acting like they think I'm having a fling with you, and I figure I'll run with that and give them what they want by taking walks and holding hands. Maybe some kind of fucking assassin's code will stop them from finding you too interesting. So, I'm afraid you'll have to put up with that for your own safety. I assure you, I have no designs on you."

She did not hide the way her face fell at these words.

Great, he thought, I expanded the problem by trying to solve it. How could she go for me?

He continued. "Mack, of course, knows a lot and will figure out the rest, but I hope not before you have devised a way to do what I need."

"Which is?"

"He's hired an ex-FBI computer cracker, trained at MIT. The guy's in Chicago with a state-of-the-art setup. Mara, Mack's daughter—you met her on the Challenger—is also savvy with the machines. The two of them are like magicians. I don't think any communication between Lithuania and Virginia will go unnoticed by them unless you can devise a way. That's your mission here. Protect the vault from Charlemagne while giving them all the information they need to kill their target."

Jade tilted her head in shock. "Kill?"

He nodded. "They're assassins, Jade. That's what they do. The target is a bad guy, don't worry, but also don't think nice guys do this work successfully, and this team is unbeaten. Stay away from them."

"But you …?"

"No. I've never killed. But I'm not one of those purists who swear he never will. If it means saving the op or the team or an innocent, hell yeah, I will. And, unlike a lot of babysitters, I have the skills."

"Babysitters?"

He raised his eyebrows in surprise. "You don't know what The Section does?"

She shook her head.

He marveled. She ran a library devoted to The Section. Had she never read any of it? But then, a lot of things were never written down.

"We provide intelligence and logistics support to the teams or individuals the government hires to take care of, shall we say, special problems," he explained. "We keep the government sanitized from such solutions. You and I are here in unacknowledged support of a wet operation. If it goes wrong, it's not only our careers at stake. It can get us killed. It's not just the target who's a nasty piece of work. Like I said, the team is just as dangerous and we're closer to them. As time goes on, they will become more volatile, more unstable, and they are very, very skilled."

SEVEN

"A woman? He has brought an American woman? Why?"

Rimas had no answer and no breath with which to speak. Kestutis had set a fast pace for this warmup run. At the end of it, the questions intensified while he took in much needed air.

"What does she look like? What is her name? Do you think she is his lover? I thought the Americans were more professional than this. The ministry has vetted him, but who is this woman?"

Rimas caught his breath, explained what he could, and stopped himself thinking about any lovers she might have.

"You took her shopping? For what?" asked Kestutis.

"Kitchen things, a good lock, and a computer. Also something for the computer that I did not recognize."

"And she has no languages?"

"She has English, of course, and also French. She attended the Sorbonne."

"The Sorbonne? And he brought her to Lithuania?"

Rimas took advantage of the time they spent stretching to ask his questions. He knew there would be no opportunity once they began sparring.

"This other American you met, the older man, what was his name?"

"Prion," said Kestutis.

"Did the ministry vet him as well? Are the two Americans working together?"

Kestutis stretched one hamstring, then the other before answering. "No, his late wife was a Lithuanian. She came home to live here after they divorced. He is very rich and wants to do something good for the country."

"By hiring fighters?"

"I suspect he wants to fight the Russians. He surveys the border with Kaliningrad. And he has brought a few American fighters as well. That is why I have been watching his compound. I thought this man Nakamura's presence might be a sign the Americans are involved, but the young woman makes me question it. Who brings a woman to such a battle?"

"American women fight, Kestutis. They are no longer restricted from combat."

"Decadent. They will soon have an army wearing high heels. Even the men."

Rimas wanted to let this go, but Kestutis would not leave it alone.

"Imagine your brother fighting the Russians," he laughed, flopping his hands on limp wrists.

Kestutis had taught him everything, how to think, how to fight, how to survive. Though he loved the man like an uncle, Rimas could not allow this to pass.

"He is my brother, Kestutis."

"He is an abomination, young man. The product of a father too weak and a mother too strong. It is well known."

"Nothing of the sort is known. Antanas and I have the same parents."

"Then you have a stronger character. That is all."

Rimas put his heart and all his strength into their sparring session and, for the first time, beat his mentor.

When Kestutis caught his breath, he said, "I want you to get close to this woman. It should not be unpleasant if she is as pretty as you say. I must know what role she is here to play."

Initially, Rimas wondered if Kestutis wanted to know if he had the same tastes as his brother, but then he remembered all information was like currency to the man. He never had enough of it.

Besides, she was certainly pretty enough to make it a pleasant task.

EIGHT

"Misha wants to know where you've been," Steve told Skosh. "You'd better go explain yourself. I'll stay and entertain Jade for you."

He gave her a suggestive smile. Everything about this guy sizzled. It reminded her of the boys she had grown up with. Only one thing on their minds, ever.

"Like hell you will, Steve," said Skosh. "Tell him I'll be right there. Let me get my coat off, for fuck's sake."

He hung his coat on the hook behind the door and pointed toward Jade, then the bedroom. He made a gesture like turning a key. She translated it as 'Go lock yourself in the bedroom.' The lock was not yet installed, but she made as if to comply and walked back to where, lo and behold, the lock was on the door. She tested it and found it fully functional. The keys, two of them, lay on the dresser. She hadn't installed it, and Skosh couldn't have, but it made her feel a little safer.

She grabbed her ditty bag from her suitcase and headed for the bathroom. It sported a small but deep freestanding tub and Jade could think of no better way to get her brain working on the puzzle Skosh had given her than by soaking her body in hot water.

Carefully locking the bathroom door, she thought it seemed a bit flimsy but figured it would at least warn her that someone was trying to come in and so give her time to throw on a towel. She soaked and luxuriated for a few minutes calling up and then rejecting one refinement after another to the problem of keeping Charlemagne out of her vault's computer. The shopping trip had given her not only an idea but also the hardware necessary to execute it.

When the water had cooled a bit, she used a toe to turn on the hot tap, supporting herself with her arms on the sides of the tub so as not to slide underwater.

The bathroom door opened. So much for that lock.

"What the fuck are you doing?" said her boss.

She saw no purpose in answering. After all, he was reasonably intelligent.

"We're on an op for chrissake. Get out of there. Now. Before somebody comes in here."

The water was deep, but it did not quite cover her breasts and there were no concealing bubbles. Maybe he heard his own voice and processed the absurdity of his words, or perhaps he finally realized what he was seeing. Either way, he turned, red-faced, and slammed the door behind him.

She did as ordered and was dry and wrapped in a towel preparing to leave when the door opened again. Sergei and Steve stood in the doorway grinning.

"A bath? On an op? Really?" This from Steve.

"If Mara did this, I would have to kill anyone who went near the door," said Sergei. "It is not good to do on an operation. Do you like the lock on your bedroom?"

"Yes, thank you, but I thought I remembered three keys."

"Correct. Misha has the third."

The conversation stalled at this point, with both men raking the towel with their eyes and Jade feeling the cold through her bare feet on a stone floor.

"Right, you two," came a voice from outside, "out of there before the babysitter has a coronary."

They scattered like magic, and she faced the scary one, Charlie. Worse, he came into the small space and closed the door behind him. He did not move, but stood there, using his eyes to x-ray behind the towel, noting every fold of it, watching her shiver, first with cold and then because of his gaze. Finally, he spoke.

"I presume Skosh has told you who we are, but did he also explain what we are?"

She nodded. He waited for more of an answer, her nod being insufficient.

"He said you are assassins." She squeaked this.

"And do you think, given our occupation, that we are what you might refer to as nice people?"

She had no way of answering this, it seemed, without increasing both her discomfort and her danger, so she did not.

"If Skosh has given you instructions and warnings regarding us, it would be wise to heed them. We are none of us incapable of forcing our attentions upon you. Your presence here, and your behavior especially, threatens to destabilize my team. I will not permit it."

He turned and opened the door. Skosh stood there tight-jawed and fists clenched.

"What did you say to her?" he said through his teeth.

Charlie's answer came slow and smooth. "Ask her. By all means, ask her."

Jade locked the bedroom door before getting dressed, while Skosh stood outside telling her to hurry up. She chose her best designer jeans, despite their having become creased in the suitcase, and a Ralph Lauren sweater that she dearly loved. She needed the mirror and lighting in the bathroom to attempt makeup, but Skosh was pretty agitated, so she simply brushed her hair and piled it on top of her head, holding it in place with a tortoiseshell comb.

She opened the door, feeling undressed without makeup.

"What did he say?" He whispered the question, so she replied in kind, repeating Charlie's words exactly. He closed his eyes and opened them slowly. "It was a threat. I'm sending you home. I'll just give them the fucking passwords to the vault."

"Hell no, you won't. I have a plan."

He did not seem to hear her but was staring at the lock on the door. "Tell me you installed this."

"No, I didn't. Sergei did."

She took the keys from the dresser, gave him one, and put the other in her pocket.

"He said somebody called Misha has the third one. Have I met him?"

"Mack. I told you, they call him Misha."

As if summoned by the reference, the man stood in spectral silence behind Skosh, who turned around when he saw her reaction.

"The caterers will soon be here, Skosh. We will be honored if you and Miss Wilmerton will join us at all mealtimes. Please bring chairs with you."

In the space of half an hour, Jade had heard a finely worded threat and a polite direct order, both of them mandatory and unambiguous.

NINE

They offered Jade a seat as far as possible away from Skosh. The courtesy with which the offer was made created a pretense that she had the option to decline, but she knew it for the fairy tale it was.

She sat next to Mack, who peppered her from time to time with slow questions, often doubling back to previous answers and pinning down all minor inconsistencies. He did not appreciate incomplete answers either, attacking every sketchy explanation she gave with terrifyingly polite tenacity.

"Where do you live?"

"I have an apartment near my library."

"Your library? What sort of library?"

"Oh, you know, just a library."

"With books?"

"Yes."

"And documents?"

The mental gymnastics required to avoid answering took too long. He smiled slightly and changed the subject.

She would have liked to listen to the general conversation in the room, but Mack was the only person speaking English. There must have been some funny jokes told, especially by Steve and Sergei. They kept up a steady banter. Even Charlie chuckled from time to time. Judging by the overall hilarity and the stony, patient look on Skosh's face, much of it was at his expense.

Twice, Jade caught herself nearly blurting out a detail about her apartment, her friends, or the job. Mack registered all near misses with that same slow smile.

Mara brought her a mug of black coffee. "Tell me, Jade," she said, "have you and Skosh been seeing each other long?"

How was she supposed to answer that? She looked at him on the other side of the small room, but Skosh didn't seem to notice her alarm. She sipped hot coffee to gain time to think of an answer, and it caught in her throat, sparking the most welcome coughing fit of her life. Mara patted her on the back to calm the cough, smiling the same slow, almost secret smile Jade had seen on Mack.

She did not eat much, but the team decimated the catered meal. There were several unpronounceable potato casserole dishes with bacon, baked chicken in a cream sauce, Brussels sprouts, sausage, sauerkraut, and fried strips of bread that looked like French fries and came with a tasty cheese dip. It all looked delicious, but Jade got precious little of it. The only thing the team consumed more of than food was coffee. She noticed Skosh was no slouch in either department.

After following the others as they placed their plates in an empty tub next to Mara's computer, she turned from there to the rug over the hole in the wall to make her escape. Charlie headed her off, taking her arm none too gently and sending her to a chair that had opened up next to Skosh.

"We will need you to attend all meetings," he said. "And I expect you to brief us about the real reason you are here, preferably without the need for torture." He smiled when he said this as if he were joking, but his eyes told her he was not.

"I don't think my assistant needs to be here," Skosh said as Jade sat next to him.

Charlie answered him with a smirk. "I think differently. We know you're up to something, Skosh, and that you think it's in support of the operation. It follows that she should hear the details directly, not as whispered pillow talk between you."

Mack opened proceedings.

"Miss Wilmerton, the name of our target is Earl Prion."

"Please, call me Jade," she said, hoping he would be less likely to kill her if they were on a first-name basis. It was becoming uncomfortably clear that these people were not playing. What had Skosh said about a knife?

"Very well, Jade," said Mack. "Prion is an American who recently came into great wealth through unknown means. He has begun to spend his money in ways that disturb your government. We have been asked to discover why he is building a small private army before we eliminate him and neutralize his force. Today, he arrived in Lithuania."

He nodded minimally at Skosh, who took up the briefing.

"My contact in Lithuanian counterintelligence, Kestutis Girdauskas, tells me Prion is recruiting locals with fighting skills, sons and grandsons of former anti-Soviet partisans, a few criminals, that sort of thing, promising money and appealing to patriotism. Americans are popular now, but not Russians. Prion has hinted that Russia is his target."

Skosh consulted a small notebook before he continued.

"Our Resident in Vilnius briefed me on the local situation. It has been just over six years since fourteen protesters were killed by Soviet troops at the TV tower in Vilnius. Russian propaganda and provocations are ongoing and are broadcast widely, along with a great many popular Russian-language cultural programs. Most Lithuanians speak at least some Russian and all educated citizens are fluent.

"The propaganda has perversely stirred peoples' memories of lionized anti-Soviet fighters, even though a few of these may have had fascist histories. Loyalties can be formed based more on emotion than reality, though there's plenty of fact to warrant it. Given Lithuanian losses under Stalin, it is perhaps understandable but does not bode well for a liberal democracy, which the people want, but their neighbor, the Bear, does not want them to have."

He put the notebook away as Mack nodded to Charlie, who turned an unwanted stare toward Jade.

"You say you are a librarian. May we assume your library is part of Skosh's organization? Don't look to him for guidance. Just answer the question."

She decided it would be unwise to lie. The man's eyes seemed to have access to every secret she had ever tried to keep.

"Yes."

"Then at least part of your reason for being here is to support our need for information?"

"Yes."

Sergei was making the rounds with a coffee pot, and Charlie paused as he held out his mug.

"Mara," said Charlie, "give Jade a notebook and pen from the FUT so she can jot down my questions." He saw the puzzled look on Jade's face and gave the definition. "Footlocker of Useful Things." Taking a long sip of coffee, he subjected her to a malign stare, or was she suspecting more malevolence than was real?

"Your list stays in this room, however," he continued in a kind of soft purr, "but you are welcome to come and refresh your memory at any time."

No, she decided, she had been *under*estimating his malice.

"I see you are catching on," he said. His lips turned up in a half smile.

Okay, this guy is beyond scary. When his smile widened even further, she promised herself she would stop thinking thoughts he could read so readily.

Charlie dictated his list as she wrote. "First, we need a place to start, a hint as to the source of Prion's funding. Your authorities must have some idea, or they would not have given us this commission. At least they should know where he banks. I want that information as soon as possible."

He swiftly piled on more questions she knew would test her system.

"Feel free to use Mara's computer to consult your database." Charlie pointed to the excellent, state-of-the-art hardware sitting on a decrepit table against one wall.

Mara turned and smiled at her. Had she not been there, Jade would have had a look at the set-up, not to send out the questions of course, but rather to get a feel for how Mara operated.

"Thank you, Mara," she said, "but I will muddle along with my notebook computer. I'm sure it will do the job."

The ambient noise of shuffling feet and sipping coffee, of occasional murmured asides in a neighbor's ear and countless audible clues to the presence of too many people gathered in a small space ceased abruptly. Only the computer behind Mara did not know any better and continued its now deafening hum in the hush. Even Skosh threw eye daggers at Jade. She beamed at them all, feigning innocence, but nobody was buying it.

Sergei broke the breathless quiet. "There was no notebook in your luggage."

This time he was the one receiving a warning frown from Charlie. He had searched her things when he installed the lock.

The lock that Mack had a key to.

TEN

"When the fuck did you acquire a notebook computer, Jade?"

"Do you ever create a sentence without using the f-word?"

Skosh snorted. Or maybe it was more of a snarl, as he squeezed her hand.

"Ow. Can't we find some other way to communicate that doesn't require us to freeze?" She peered down at the ice under the dock they were standing on.

"No, we can't, unless you want to take Charlie's suggestion and go whisper pillow talk."

She had already decided such a necessity would make her very happy indeed but sighed when he continued without pause.

"It would be completely unsecure anyway. No doubt Pavlenko has half a dozen devices planted around your mattress. It's hard enough trying to keep an eye out for a directional microphone out here; we'll never find all the touches he has set. I hope you've been inspecting your pockets. Also, check the lining of your coat before we go out on our oh-so-romantic walks. Fuck, it's freezing out here. Now tell me your plan and how you got this computer."

He pointed to the bag slung over her shoulder. He had made her bring it with them. She objected at first, but the memory of Charlie's smile came to mind, and she stopped mid-protest. The new suggestion that Sergei may have hidden bugs around her pillow convinced her further, at least until she could come up with a system that would alert her to tampering.

"I bought it at that computer shop," she said. "It's a Pentium and I got it for an excellent price. I'll use it to get the answers they need."

Skosh's glare seemed a tad belligerent.

"How?"

She returned the belligerence with an extra frown as interest.

"By using a system and a decoy. Do you still have that encryption modem you took from me this afternoon? You put it in your pocket."

He handed it back to her. "Explain."

"Rimas and I had lunch at his brother's apartment. I borrowed the phone—and paid him for it, of course—and called my assistant, Dennis. He has a key to my apartment."

"He?"

"Yes. He."

"Why does he have a key to your place?"

She refrained from telling him it was none of his business and chose instead to serve him the silence the question deserved.

But he was not satisfied.

"You're sleeping with your assistant? You know that's wrong, right?"

She stopped and tilted her head at this preposterous statement. "Why would it be wrong?"

"Because of the power difference."

"He hasn't forced himself on me." She turned away from him, unwilling to let him see her blush.

He held her upper arm to keep her facing him. "Not him. You. You have too much power over him to make it a truly consensual relationship."

"All couples share power in different ways. If he and I were in such a relationship—and mind you, I'm not saying we are—I couldn't possibly be more powerful. He's almost as tall as you." Though nowhere near as fit, she thought.

"Can you fire him?"

Her argument crashed to the ground.

"It never occurred to me," she whispered.

Jade was new to the concept of having power. In the Army, her biggest job had been as an assistant to a colonel. He had the power. No one ever reported to her. Now in the vault, she held the livelihoods of five people in her hands. Skosh watched her face as thought followed thought. She looked up at him, mortified.

"Dennis is gay," she said finally. "He takes care of my cat when I travel. I made arrangements with him to use email to check up on the cat and told him to use my old notebook. It has the same encryption device. I will use it to get the answers to Charlie's questions."

Jade could have sworn Skosh was fighting a smile until he glanced over her shoulder and rolled his eyes. She was about to turn to look behind her when he took her chin, tilted it up, and kissed her. Seriously. Surprise opened her eyes. The cold made them tear. His eyes were open, too, but were looking past her. How very disappointing, but she closed her eyes and enjoyed what it could have been.

"So is this the power difference you guys were discussing? Feeling guilty are we, Skosh?"

He broke off the kiss. "Fuck off, Donovan."

"This is a shit detail, Skosh, having to follow you around the frozen North with a directional. How about you just go tell Misha what you're really up to, so I don't have to freeze my ass off every time you want to brief your assistant."

"A little privacy goes a long way, Steve."

"So does a little information. It's time you provided it." Steve took Jade's arm and turned her toward him. "What's this in your hand?"

"Hands off her," said Skosh.

"Make me."

"Gladly."

During this rather electric exchange, Jade put the modem in her pocket, acting secretive and making sure Steve noticed. The pause gave Skosh a chance to hit him and send the parabolic microphone he had been carrying sliding along the peer. Skosh soon followed it onto the concrete, courtesy of Steve's fist, but he came up whirling a long-legged kick through the air before Steve could close the distance enough to punch again. Steve took the blow from Skosh's foot to his midsection like it never happened and would have replied in kind, but all three of them became aware of an audience at the same moment.

They turned to face Mack, standing hatless in the cold wind under a path light in the dusk. No one had seen or heard him approach. He invited them to precede him to the house with a minimal sweep of one hand.

ELEVEN

At first, Skosh was more concerned Mack had allowed Steve to enter the smaller safehouse, unsupervised, with Jade. He knew Donovan too well to trust him alone with a pretty woman. Presumably, Mack also knew Donovan's habits better than anybody else. Skosh was surprised, then, as he pulled him to the back of the house.

"Really, Mack? Literally hauling me behind the fucking woodshed? Isn't that a bit old fash...."

Mack's fist pounded into his gut, arresting the word mid-larynx. Skosh struggled for breath as Mack shoved him up against the shed wall with a twisting grip on his coat collar.

"How dare you strike a member of my team."

The tone was low and almost conversational, but punctuated by increased pain as Mack tightened his grip on Skosh's throat. He continued.

"Touch one of them again and I promise you a slow and painful death. Now, you will explain to me why you are not yourself."

He loosened the twist sufficiently for Skosh to catch enough air to speak. Unfortunately, the labyrinth of his problems disoriented him, making the response too slow for Mack's purposes.

Mack twisted the collar again.

"Tell me!"

"I… I can't. It has nothing to do with the operation. It is my problem alone. I.…"

"Who has set you up?"

Skosh had known since childhood that the inscrutable Asian thing was a myth because he had never managed to pull it off.

This time was no exception. Not only did Mack read his surprise accurately, but he then leapt to the heart of the problem with Mack-like accuracy and hissed a demand.

"There is a woman involved. But it is not this woman, Jade. I want her name."

"I can't. Ethical.…"

"Ethics? You put us all at risk and plead ethics as your reason? You work in the most unethical section of a largely unethical organization within the government of an historically unethical nation and you pretend to be behaving ethically?"

Skosh had never before been the recipient of this kind of slow, concentrated anger. Because it came from a famously efficient killer, it helped him find his own steel core. He would not die sniveling. It gave him the strength to look into those blue eyes, though he was careful to filter out any suggestion of insolence.

"I cannot divulge details of my organization, Mack, and my conscience will not allow me to put an innocent, no matter how ignorant, in danger."

Mack's eyebrows rose in surprise. He released his hold and pointed toward the house.

"Instead, you brought that innocent into the heart of danger. A librarian, no less. An attractive one."

"That was not the plan, as you well know."

"Do you know what will happen to you if you fail?"

Skosh wondered briefly which of several failures Mack was referring to, but he knew all the outcomes and relished none of them. He answered simply, "Yes."

"Does she know what will happen to her?" Mack gestured again toward the house.

Skosh had no answer.

With a hard shove, Mack sent him sprawling over the stacked firewood.

"I will know who and why and where, Skosh, with or without your cooperation, and I will take action to protect my interests. It is time for you to adopt my interests as your own. There is a large difference between damaging your career and losing your life."

TWELVE

Jade was not present for the great chewing out of her boss. Fairness would dictate that Steve also should get a tongue lashing, but she noticed a bruise on Skosh's cheek when he came back and never saw one on Steve. There were more bruises on Skosh's abdomen. She noticed them when he changed into a set of black cold-weather clothing in the kitchen.

She did her best not to enjoy the view, but some things are impossible.

"We are all headed out to recce the target," he told her as he inserted an earbud and ran the wire to a small radio attached to his belt. "Both safe-houses will be locked and the sensors around the perimeter are working. Lock yourself in the bedroom and don't move. You should be safe enough this early in the op."

"I have to get answers to Charlie's questions," she reminded him.

He stared at her. She pointed to the notebook on the kitchen table. He mouthed 'be careful' without sound and said aloud, "Do it quick and then lock yourself in. We won't be long."

It took her no more than half an hour, and that included the phone call to Dennis's cellular phone. She shut down the computer, hid the modem in her pillow, and locked the bedroom door behind her as she crept to the hole in the wall and nudged the carpet aside.

A dim light glowed in one corner of the main downstairs room. Jade was grateful for it as she focused on her objective. She would have barked her shin on a footlocker had the room been totally dark. As she reached her right hand behind the CPU of Mara's computer and felt for the power switch, she became aware of a feeling. A presence. It reminded her of a ghost movie when the heroine gets all goose-pimply just before a hideous ghoul jumps out at her.

This was much worse.

She stood straight, turned slowly, and faced Mack. Again, the minimal gesture to precede him. He pointed to a chair until she sat down in it, then sat in the one facing her. So far, despite no words being spoken and no weapons brandished, she felt the presence of danger. He stayed close to her in a way she knew he meant as a threat. He seemed ready at any moment to escalate the situation.

"I see you have an interest in computers, Jade."

"Yes, Sir." Now, what would be the use in denying it? She ventured to look at him, doing her best not to show her fear. In the low light from the table lamp next to her, his face was partially shaded and what she knew to be grey hair at the temples appeared blond. His skin showed some years, she supposed, but it also gave her a good idea of what he looked like when he was her age. He had rolled up the sleeves of his white shirt and removed his tie. He wore a gun in a shoulder holster. She swallowed hard and he spoke again.

"I am amazed that so small a machine has become important to our survival."

This was not her idea of conversation. Instinct told her not to pry and self-preservation counseled silence.

After almost a minute, during which time she steeled herself to meet his gaze, he said, "I see that my words perplex you. Are you unaware that Skosh's mistake has imperiled your survival?"

She wondered if he could see her wide eyes in the dim light, or if he could hear the pounding of her heart. She could.

"Perhaps you harbor the illusion that you are safe with us?" he added in a low voice.

She sucked in her breath audibly.

"Good. You are no longer deceived. Now, I will explain my position. I know that Skosh has made a mistake."

She wondered how he would explain this conclusion and remembered Skosh's comment that somebody named Penelope should be old and wearing sensible shoes.

Mack resumed. "Every man on the team is now married, but except for Sergei, none of us is incapable of taking advantage of a propitious situation."

What a way with language this guy had.

"Sergei would be more likely than most to avail himself of such an opportunity. He had a deplorable reputation in the KGB, but he knows Mara would kill him. Skosh understands us. He is experienced with other teams and has been trained in his present position by a man who has known us for thirty years. He would not bring a young, attractive woman into our proximity. At least not for purposes other than …"

He let the thought drop without naming it. She was grateful. His long pause made her think he might expect a comment from her, but when he began again, she realized he had been carefully arranging his words.

"Perhaps your real name is ambiguous. It may appear to be male. From the list of possible candidates we have assembled, however, I think it more likely that he thought you to be considerably older. Either way, Skosh now realizes his mistake, and it has deranged him. He hit Steve this evening, a reckless act very unlike him. Luckily, Steve saw me before he could kill him outright."

In all this time, the man barely moved, yet Jade was never unaware that he'd be pretty speedy in any direction, and she was directly in front of him. She didn't know if he noticed how firm a grasp she had on the arms of her chair. Foolishly, she hoped everybody would return immediately and the noise and bustle would take his mind off his intentions, whatever they were.

What had caused her mere serious concern was well on its way to becoming terror and he was not finished producing more of it. He continued.

"Skosh is a very good babysitter, and we need him on this operation. It is too late and too difficult to replace him with someone as competent. Your presence, then, threatens the success of the operation and therefore our lives. My normal response would be to shoot you immediately, but I fear this would worsen Skosh's derangement and make him a liability as well. I hope you understand how tenuous your fate remains."

He tilted his head, expecting a response for the first time.

She managed a hoarse whisper. "I do."

"I will not ask you to tell me your real purpose here. You are the subordinate, and such a revelation would be a betrayal of your superior. We will give you and Skosh sufficient privacy for you to repeat to him what I have said. I will leave it to him to discuss the topic with me."

The team returned at this point, noisy, muddy, and sweating despite the cold, and Jade felt a tidal wave of joy and relief until Mack said, "Whatever system you have devised to obtain the answers to Charlie's questions should have borne fruit by now. If it has not, your method is unacceptable."

With that dismissal, she lost no time in slipping through the rug under cover of the chaos filling the room.

THIRTEEN

Skosh turned, the kitchen phone in his hand. "Where the fuck did you come from?"

He had to ask though the answer was pretty obvious. The rug behind Jade still swayed.

"I need that phone line to download the answers," she said as she headed for the bedroom to fetch the modem. He followed her.

"I thought I was pretty clear. What were you doing over there? Mack was there. He stayed behind. Don't tell me you went over there for some incredibly dumb reason. He didn't come over here, did he? He didn't …"

They were interrupted by Steve, disheveled and panting, his face still blackened by camo paint. The brown eyes were unmistakable or Skosh would have thought he was Sergei. He leaned against the door jamb, smirking.

"Lover's tiff?"

"Get the fuck out of here, Donovan."

"You going to hit me again if I don't, Skosh?"

He did not answer because he was counting to ten.

Steve spoke again. "Misha told me to assure you that the devices in this house are turned off. He gives you his word. Ask him directly, if you don't believe me." He tilted his head. "What's that?"

"I believe you. I don't have time to deal with your devices right now. My Lithuanian counterpart will be here any minute because of what you left behind out there."

"Not my work, Skosh."

"One of your methods, though."

"It's not like I have a patent on it."

"Get out of here before Kestutis sees you."

Skosh slipped outside the front door and made a show of locking it with his key, pretending no one else was inside. *I'm good at my job. I'm experienced. Why am I unraveling?*

Kestutis stood waiting on the sidewalk.

They took the Lithuanian agent's government car because this was an official meeting, and because Skosh did not want the man anywhere near a vehicle that might be used by the team. The two did not speak as they drove toward Nida at the southern end of the Lithuanian portion of the Spit.

Skosh used the time to examine the peril he was in and how uncommonly off his game he had become in the past few days. The past week. He should have read that commission much earlier and not waited until the night before he was to leave. Why didn't he? He knew why. He had been busy fending off Candace.

Kestutis pulled onto a narrow forest track as Skosh pointed to it. It ended abruptly a few hundred yards in, and they got out to walk, still without speaking. Skosh led the way.

As he pushed aside tree branches, he remembered he didn't get the damned commission until late that evening. That was unusual. Timing was not as critical for this op, but administrative delays were always frowned upon. He briefly wondered if she had anything to do with processing that commission. She was high enough in the hierarchy. Surely, a woman wouldn't use her position for revenge, would she?

Skosh tripped on the tree root that told him they were close, but he kept his balance, turned sixty degrees right, and saw the opening in a shaft of moonlight.

"The man is dead," said Kestustis.

Biting back a sarcastic reply, Skosh said nothing. He liked his Lithuanian counterpart but did not trust him enough to venture too much friendliness.

"You just came across the body?" There was the tiniest bit of irony in Kestutis's tone.

Skosh nodded, wondering if it was friendly sarcasm, or otherwise.

A muscular man in middle age, Kestutis moved quietly through the brush on the forest floor. He nudged the body with the toe of one boot, then grabbed a shoulder and heaved the corpse onto its back. The dead man stared unseeing at the moon. The neck bulged unnaturally to one side, betraying the cause of death, but spots of blood glistened on the jacket, and the forest floor all around had been trampled. Kestutis searched the jacket pockets and handed Skosh an American passport.

"One of yours?"

Skosh examined the document while Kestutis opened the jacket and shirt, revealing an abdominal stab wound and a great many tattoos. A flashlight confirmed that most of these were gang tattoos, probably done in prison.

The Lithuanian official waited for a reply.

"Not one of our best, shall we say," said Skosh. "He must have met with an accident."

Surely, Kestutis would be astute enough to know the rules of this game.

"I see. I will take you back to your house, Skosh. I can find this place again in the morning. Thank you for alerting me."

When he returned to the safehouse, Skosh lay beside Jade on the bed for the purportedly private briefing Mack had both promised and demanded of them earlier. He noticed with regret that she seemed indifferent to his proximity. He felt anything but indifferent to hers.

They lay on top of the duvet, fully clothed and filthy. Well, he was filthy. Also cold, disheveled and dispirited. At least she didn't have mud in her hair. He knew she would have liked a bath but hoped she finally understood that was a thing of the past. He would have told her how attractive she remained despite the snarls in that magnificent hair, but it would have been inappropriate and unprofessional, and he refused to make yet another mistake this trip.

"Charlie was pleased with the answers," she said before he could ask.

"Did they get into the vault?"

"No, there is no connection to the vault."

"But the information comes from there, doesn't it?"

"Yes, but by way of a clean floppy each time. Dennis is using my old portable computer and the reception desk phone line, not the T-1 at the vault."

He turned his head toward her and whispered. "Why the encryption?"

"To keep their hacker busy for a while and protect the classified."

"With an old modem?"

"It's good enough up to Secret, and so far that's as high as the information has been, though there have been some sensitive sources. Because my old laptop has the same modem, the data is encrypted end to end. Even when—not if—the former FBI guy...." she turned her head to look at him, eyebrows up in a question mark.

"Justin."

"Justin, then. Even when he breaks it, it won't matter because they'll only see what they're already getting from me."

He found her hand and squeezed it.

"Thank you."

He took a few deep breaths and asked about her conversation with Mack.

"I'm sorry," he said when she finished.

She didn't answer. He realized nothing she could say would make him feel better, and pretty much anything it was possible to say would be more likely to make him feel worse. She simply squeezed his hand back.

He smiled, relieved, and fell asleep within two breaths.

When he jumped off the bed shortly before dawn, Skosh did his best not to wake her but failed. She sat up, blinking in the overhead light. Sergei stood in the doorway.

"What, Sergei?" he said, annoyed.

"Misha said to tell you devices are back on, and he expects you to speak to him now."

Jade was busy trying to free her hair from a decorative comb that had been overwhelmed by her new reality. She met Skosh's look and gave a slight nod that he understood meant it was safe to tell Mack the real reason he had brought her.

The man would take it out of his hide again, Skosh knew, but it would be a mistake not to tell him. And he was done making mistakes. At any cost.

FOURTEEN

J ade poured a fresh mug of coffee and handed it to Skosh when he returned from his meeting with Mack. He winked at her, put the mug on the kitchen table, and hugged her, whispering an operational sweet nothing into her ear.

"Mack is pissed. Well done."

On the one hand, her boss was happy. On the other, the man who had threatened her was not.

Skosh pulled a blood-smeared American passport out of a pocket and handed it to her.

"I need to know everything we have on this guy."

She accepted it with her fingertips and dropped it on the table immediately. Acutely conscious of the inadequate bathroom lock, she had managed to wash her face and hands and had run a toothbrush briefly over her teeth. Blood was not on the list of substances she found acceptable to dabble in that morning. The passport sat next to their coffee, so she moved the mugs lest they be contaminated.

"Well, come on," said Skosh. "Get going. Put it in with the list Charlie gave you this morning."

Jade tried to remember a list. She did remember Charlie. He was difficult to forget, entering the bathroom as he did when the toothbrush had only just begun to dispel the fuzz of a luxurious three hours of sleep. She had spat at the mirror in panic.

At Skosh's mention of a list, Jade dashed into the bedroom and dug into her suitcase, locating yesterday's crumpled pair of jeans, the ones she had slept in—the ones she had put on despite a crease, a mere crease, from the suitcase. There was indeed a slip of paper in one back pocket. Tiny, cramped writing filled a torn section of Sergei's unmistakable lined paper from the FUT. She was going to need a magnifying glass. After retrieving her notebook computer and the encryption modem, she headed back to the kitchen table.

The coffee in her mug had gone cold.

At breakfast, Mack gave her a few of the slow gazes that seemed to be his specialty. He was letting her know he noticed her, that he was displeased with her, and that he was still tempted to kill her. She accepted the danger with a tinge of pride because she had beaten him in such a small way using old technology. Perhaps he would come to respect her. Then again, maybe water flows naturally uphill, emptying the sea.

Mara sat down next to Jade, grinning. She spoke softly, out of the side of her mouth while nibbling a piece of toast. "You have bested Misha. That is excellent but do be careful. He can be dangerous."

Can be? Jade wished she could shout this question with full sarcasm.

"I think I know your method," Mara continued. "It appears to be insurmountable. Even the telephone call to your assistant gives us nothing. Tell me, should I care about the encryption?"

Jade was tempted to thank her for her kindness by telling her not to bother, but she had decided she would give no quarter. She could not know what or when something would create more danger for herself or Skosh. Responding with a quiet shrug, she did her best to look enigmatic. Mara widened her grin.

The grin fell as Charlie stood before them.

"What is it, Charlie?" Mara asked.

He tilted his chin; she sighed, took her plate, and moved away with an apologetic smile. As he sat beside her, Jade felt cold tension run up her spine.

"You should lock the bathroom door when you're in there," he said.

"I did."

She refrained from pointing out that it was the bathroom in Skosh's safehouse, not in his, and that he knew she was in there because he had been looking for her. She was pretty sure a properly working lock would not have stopped him.

"It is faulty then," he said as if that had been in question. "I will ask Sergei to look at it." He turned his head and smiled at her. Not a full, genuine smile, but a seductive one, full of suggestion. "Then you can resume your baths in safety."

If she had any illusion that the word safety meant the same thing to Charlie as it did to her, it was dispelled by the look of wide-eyed alarm on Skosh's face across the room. He swallowed quickly, took his half-full plate to the container on the table, and tossed his head toward the hole in the wall. It was an order to follow him ASAP.

"Excuse me," she told Charlie, trying to stand.

He held her by the arm. "Skosh will wait. He cannot afford to confront me. I'll tell Sergei to fix the lock."

He let go with the same meaningful smile, and she skedaddled through the hole in the wall. Grabbing the modem from the kitchen table, she slipped it into her pocket as Skosh pulled her out the door.

FIFTEEN

"He terrifies me, Skosh."

"That's probably his intention."

"Why? He must know I get it. I don't need those icy eyes reminding me he's dangerous."

They had walked for some time before Skosh asked her about her conversation with Charlie. She recounted it, word for word, doing her best not to let her voice shake. When they reached the center of a small parking lot with a clear view all around them, Skosh stopped to face her, stamping his feet against the cold. His breath made little clouds as he spoke.

"He could be just scratching an itch. Such things are possible. You are an attractive woman, and your hair is almost the same shade of deep auburn as his wife's, but when he's on an operation, Charlie is more like one of your computers. Everything is programmed; all actions have purpose. He has a reason for scaring you that way. That's not to say he won't follow through and try to seduce you, so beware, but if he does, he will have some other more primary agenda, even if enjoyment is a side benefit."

"What agenda?" *And whose enjoyment?* She was pretty sure it would not be hers.

"My guess is he wants to break your system for keeping them out of the vault. It's been a while since they helped themselves to our information."

"They had access?"

"Several times over the years. So have many others, especially once the bulk of our files were computerized. It used to be everybody had to recruit and pay traitors and spies. Now they just hire the Justins of this world."

"The answer to the Justins of the world," she said, "is the Dennises of the world. Good old-fashioned legwork, but with an electronic vector."

"You're sure they can't find a way in?"

"Not with the information we provide, no. There is no communication between the files we receive from Dennis and the computer itself. If they find a back door, it won't be because they asked where Prion banks."

"You found that?"

She nodded. "Turns out it's a German bank called Felixsee. I was surprised. I think Mack was, too. Tell me about your, um, interview with him. What did he ask you?"

Skosh took a deep breath. It was a simple, inadvertent indication of the strain he was under and reminded her that for him, Mack was more than a threat. He was a reality. She caught a glimpse of her own situation in that inverted sigh and shivered.

He took her arm and led her down the street instead of out to the pier. His cloud of words condensed in the air.

"Mack repeated the theory of my 'mistake' that he explained to you. I did my best not to let on that he was right, but he's such an arrogant son of a bitch, I'm sure he took it for granted."

"Then I am a mistake?"

She was not sure how she felt about this, but it made her uncomfortable.

"That is the fiction Mack is maintaining. It is at least half true. He is also dead-on correct that I should send you home, but I can't."

She looked up at him, puzzled. He stopped and frowned.

"I guess I owe you the truth."

Jade wondered which portion of whose truth she was about to hear.

Skosh released another sigh and began walking again. She noticed he did not check the vicinity for lurkers with listening devices. They must have been granted another period of privacy, she decided, and Steve had the luxury of staying warm inside.

Starting with a few ums and ahs, Skosh tried to find the words he needed to convey his version of the past two days. Jade waited, ready to sift it through the many bullshit filters these people had been teaching her during the last day and a half.

"I didn't get the full copy of the commission until late in the evening we flew out," he began. "I read it before turning in. The team was due in-country in two days' time, and I expected to fly out in the morning. I don't think Mack thought I would read it, but I always do, and it's almost always standard. This time it wasn't."

"What was wrong with it?" Jade wondered how, exactly such things were done, who signed them, and where the documents were stored. They were not in her vault.

Skosh turned back toward the house.

"I don't want to stray too far," he said. "Last night's corpse displayed a few unsavory tattoos. There are likely to be more of those guys not far enough away.

"When I read the commission, I noticed a stipulation that I was to provide access to any necessary information kept in The Section's database."

"Did it define necessary?"

"No. That would be covered in a general provision that says the team leader has the final say in all such questions."

"I see."

What Jade could see was that Mack knew how to play chess.

Skosh continued. "I called Brent in personnel and got a list of people who could act as an in-country liaison with the vault. I needed someone who could connect with the vault's computer without letting Justin piggyback into the system."

"And you picked an old woman with sensible shoes named Penelope."

It took him a moment to answer. She decided the hesitation came from embarrassment, a possible sign of truth.

"Ye-es," he said. "I made a few quiet arrangements, booking us on separate airlines. Then Claire called while I was packing and told me she was about to land, and did I understand I was to ride with her? I think Mack must have launched her earlier in the day. He knew what I was doing before I had thought of it."

"Now you're saying he knows you always read the commissions? You just said he didn't know that."

"He reads minds, like I told you yesterday. But I had to stick to my plan to bring Penelope out here. I didn't have any backup strategy. I had just closed my suitcase when the airline called. Penelope's reservation had been canceled. Okay, I thought, I'll take her with me. He won't think anything of me bringing an old secretary to arrange catering, so I proceeded with the plan knowing full well Claire would radio ahead.

"When the lights came on in the cabin, I saw you and knew I was sunk. He wasn't going to buy it, and on top of that, I had brought a desirable young woman into the midst of what I know is a gang of amoral reprobates. Last night, Mack reminded me about all of this in the choicest language you can imagine. As Steve would say, he tore me a new one."

"Do you mean he was concerned about my safety?" It did not seem to fit with Jade's overall impression of the man.

"Oh, no. He repeated what he said on the Challenger. He is still not sure he will risk anything to protect you. You see, if something happens to you, I will have to give him access to the vault's computer in order to abide by the agreement. There is no other choice. It would be limited access, but that's all Justin needs."

"But if you refuse?"

"That would be an act of seppuku."

"Suicide? How?"

"Without the information, the team will pull out, making the operation fail. An unexplained pull-out would damage their reputation, giving them no choice but to make sure the world knows whose fault it was. They'll publish the agreement and kill the babysitter. They'll be sorry about it, no doubt, but I'll be too dead to enjoy their regret."

She gasped and stopped to look at him, stunned. Grabbing his sleeve with one pink mitten, she turned him toward her, wishing with everything she had that the moment was filled with romantic magic in a sunny location and not deadly reality in the frozen North.

"He made a quiet move," she said, "then when you tried a similar move, he interfered by canceling the hotel. Now he has pinned me with a direct threat to you. I protect the vault, your king. It is a fork as well."

He wrinkled his brow.

"He's playing chess, Skosh."

Jade was dismayed by the familiar look on Skosh's face, the dawning realization that she had a brain. She felt flattered that he had found her appealing enough to be blinded by attraction, but usually when she betrayed her intellect, it spelled the end of any interest. It wasn't like she could turn it off and keep only the feminine appearance part of her whole self.

He hesitated with more apparent confusion than concern, visibly masking it with a return to business.

"There is one more thing I should tell you, Jade. Mack complained that your answers to their questions are too slow and too heavily redacted. He is turning up the heat. But then, so is Prion. Were you able to get the information Charlie asked for? And what about that passport I gave you?"

One of the best things about having had military training was that it taught her to simply shut up when her boss pressed her for a result that he was, himself, at that very moment preventing her from attaining.

"It will be there when we go inside," she said.

She fervently hoped so as they reached the door.

SIXTEEN

At first, Misha winced as he and Michael walked toward the pier but with every step the pain became easier. *I was a fool to let them goad me into that fight*, he thought. Each injury takes longer to heal. How long this time? Three weeks. Unacceptable.

He glanced to the side. Michael had not seen the wince. Good. He did not need nagging from his son. Alex was perfectly capable of annoying him all on her own.

"Has Justin found a way into their system yet?" he asked.

"No."

Michael's jaw was set. The sight of it reminded Misha that he was grinding his own teeth. He consciously relaxed but could not help stewing over being thwarted by a young American woman without sense enough to dress appropriately.

"But I think I know how she does it," said Michael, "and have taken steps."

Misha nodded, wondering what it was he considered appropriate dress. Was he so old he could criticize a tight sweater on a pretty woman? Mara did not wear such things in these conditions. She had better sense. No, she didn't, he realized. She had a husband who would kill a man for looking at her too long. Misha was glad of it. It meant he did not have to.

"She is completely unqualified to be here," said Michael. "Skosh has lost his mind."

"But she found a way to block Justin."

Misha stared out over the lagoon toward Klaipeda and watched the thoughts his mind had conjured. Why, exactly, was he bothered? The woman had no protection. Well, she had Skosh. Could he? According to his information, he could. Would he? He allowed his mind to explore the question.

Michael cleared his throat. "Justin broke into the computer at Prion's German bank."

Misha stopped his calculations and waited for more.

"Prion sent a letter to a bank officer thanking him for meeting with him in Manhattan. According to the letter, they had enjoyed a long conversation over whiskey and cigars that planted the seeds of an idea, and would he like to hear it?"

"Did the officer reply?"

"There is no reply in the file. But not long afterward, the bank approved a loan for several million dollars."

"Is Justin looking elsewhere?"

"He found quite a few internet forums where Prion is active. He uses various aliases to rally men to one cause or another."

"Men?"

"Yes. All of them are men, or pretend to be, though I cannot imagine a woman would want to discuss such topics. Justin sent me samples. Mostly frank discussions about women, weapons, street fighting, that kind of thing. Prion gave a contact email to several men he met on these forums."

"And the loan? How much has he spent? Where?"

"He has drawn only about half of it so far, mostly in cash. There is the compound at the southern end of the spit near Nida. He paid cash for the land after possibly paying bribes to be allowed to build there— primarily wooden huts. He brings in shipments of packaged foods, much like field rations, by truck from Germany. He is loose with this kind of information, but careful where it counts."

"How so?" Misha shifted his gaze back to Klaipeda as he listened.

"Large sums of cash are unaccounted for. Justin could find nothing, but I read again through every internet discussion that ended with contact information and one of the conversations about weaponry dealt specifically with small arms, tactical explosives, and equipment for light infantry. Prion gave his email at the end of it. Justin is working on getting into it."

"So, an arms dealer."

Michael nodded. "One more thing about that conversation, Papa. Prion began it by saying his banker had recommended the forum they were on."

Misha studied the white sky, the cranes at the port, the steel-grey lagoon.

"Increase the pressure, Michael. Who is this banker? And what weapons dealer did he recommend? It will tell us who is behind this. The Americans know or they would not have offered the commission. Damn them."

"The verification …"

"Was partial," interrupted Misha. "It contained only Prion's recruitment efforts. The information clause was meant to complete it. The bastards are jeopardizing this op to keep us from information we will need now and for the future."

"Skosh is already unhinged."

"Dismantle him completely then. Use the woman. There is no one to protect her and he knows it."

SEVENTEEN

Dennis had failed her. Lucky for Jade, another meeting started just then, and she used the chaos that begins most meetings, even ones chaired by scary people like Charlie, to call her assistant.

"What the hell, Dennis?"

She put plenty of urgency in her voice even before she felt Charlie's looming presence way too close behind her. She turned and looked up at his smug half-smile as she heard Dennis tell her all about the hell.

"Okay," she said into the phone. "Do what you can, please."

Urgency was replaced by defeat. She hung up the phone and turned back to Charlie.

"That's dirty," she said, closing her eyes immediately and wishing she could take back the complaint, regretting that she gave him the satisfaction of acknowledging his victory.

Charlie held the rug aside for her and pointed to the chair next to Mack.

Meetings were not new to Jade. If it's true an Army marches on its stomach, then the menu is planned in a meeting. Make that a series of meetings. When she had worked for the colonel, she was required to attend all staff meetings. She never had a speaking part but took copious notes because she was the invisible one, responsible for researching solutions and drafting instructions after the brass were done complaining. Here, she was sure the same concepts applied. The attendees had changed into suits and ties—the uniform of civilians with serious business.

Jade sat down next to Mack wishing she had paper and pen because she expected to be required to remember a long series of ramblings disguised as reports. The meeting opened in silence. Busy noticing a regrettable shiny spot on her right suede half-boot, she did not register the lack of reports and complaints that should have been droning on in the background noise of her attention. But she felt the uncomfortable gaze of the man next to her. Jade hoped she was imagining it and threw a sideways glance in that direction to confirm she was as invisible in this as well as in every other meeting she ever had the misfortune to attend.

He caught the glance and held it. Those eyes were very blue. Alien, she would say, because they contained none of the usual reactions to her, no indications of repulsion or attraction, compassion or disdain, curiosity or indifference. She could call that look hostile, but even that would be less than accurate because hostility is an emotion. Jade stared into the eyes of a big cat who was not particularly hungry at the moment but would either walk away or attack based on an algorithm she had no hope of discerning.

Skosh cleared his throat to break the silence. "Did you bring the information, Jade?"

He knew damn well she hadn't. She had walked in empty-handed. She welcomed the question nonetheless because it broke the spell and told her what they were waiting for.

As she launched an explanation, doing her best not to whine, she laid the blame squarely on Charlie by looking at him as she gave her excuses.

"Dennis had to find four tires and that at midnight, no less, but he has done so, and I expect to receive his report momentarily. I should probably check on that now. I think the malicious damage to Dennis's car was unconscionable as well as unforeseeable."

She did not expect a reply and did not want one. Jade was playing a tactical game of defiance and thought she was holding her own. Her belligerent glare made her point for her, but Charlie answered her words in a purr.

"Surely not as unconscionable as malicious damage to Dennis himself would be."

Jade realized suddenly that while she moved plastic checkers around a paper board, Charlie played three-dimensional chess with live bodies in an alien world. This was a skewer, with Dennis directly threatened while she was the true target behind the attack. Charlie sat as still and emotionless as a computer, giving nothing away. The purr, his words, and his stillness left her breathless until Mara tried to rescue her.

"You should bring your new notebook in here," said the equally alien young woman. "You can connect it on our telephone line and watch for

Dennis's email with the information. Why don't you go get it now?"

Jade stared at her, blinking.

"It will be just the same as consulting your computer on your line, Jade. We have been watching everything on that line anyway. It makes no difference to your excellent system."

Jade wanted an excuse to leave the room. She needed to stand alone in that tiny kitchen beyond the hanging rug and let her body shake for a little while. But her legs refused the order to stand, and her feet did not move. Sergei got up, went through the rug, and came back with the notebook. He handed it to her along with the encryption modem. She had hidden the device carefully in what she thought was a secret place behind the locked door of her bedroom.

Consciousness relies on breath. She had neglected this fact for too long and promptly passed out.

The shouted f-words in various voices helped bring her around immediately when her body's autonomic system sucked in the required air as she slid off her chair and onto the floor, still sitting up. Skosh loomed over her.

"What the fuck, Skosh?" came a voice. "Not only did you bring a librarian, but one that fucking faints."

She recognized the soft southern accent of Steve.

"What the hell did you say to her, Pavlenko?" This came from Skosh.

"I said nothing. I give her computer. That's all."

"You must realize this is not going to work, Skosh." The purr was unmistakable.

"Not if you're going to fucking terrify her every five minutes, Charlie, and then you add her assistant to your scary-as-shit threat list."

"Jade! Jade! Look at me." It was a woman's voice.

She managed to focus on the person in front of her. Mara held her hand and patted her wrist in the time-honored tradition of bringing around a swooning female. Jade gave her an embarrassed smile.

Skosh pulled her to a stand and turned to Mack, who had not moved from the chair next to her.

"I need fifteen minutes."

Mack nodded almost imperceptibly toward Sergei, presumably signaling that he should turn off the listening devices.

Skosh pushed her through the crowd, through the rug, and toward her room, where he had to unlock the door. Sergei had thoughtfully locked it again after raiding it for her modem. Nothing seemed out of place. Except the modem. That was now in Mara's hands.

They stood beside the dresser. Jade hung her head and could not look up at Skosh. She knew he wanted to send her back and that such an act would cost him everything. Fighting tears, she was determined not to add yet another weak-looking reaction to the repertoire of Jade-The-Unsuitable.

Skosh lifted her chin as she manufactured a pretend strength, dry-eyed and, she hoped, dignified. Total honesty presented itself as the only reasonable solution. Well, almost total. She wouldn't confess how much she still wanted him.

"I'm so out of my depth, Skosh. Please, give me time."

EIGHTEEN

"**Y**our assistant has sent you the information," Mara told her as Jade took the seat next to Mack ten minutes later. "But I cannot decipher it because I do not have the key."

Jade counted carefully and winced. The next key contained a word, but there was no way to avoid giving it.

"A-B-A-R-E-O."

Mara typed it in and the printer next to her computer went into action.

Mack looked at the printout first, then handed it to Jade, indicating that she should read it aloud.

"Prion's wealth appears to be based on debt," she read, as steadily as she could. "It is a secured debt, but Felixsee Bank refuses to allow US authorities access to the loan documents."

"Mara," said Mack, giving her a pointed glance. She turned to her keyboard.

Jade continued with the answer to the morning's second question. "The dead man went by the alias Bert Badass. His real name was Bernard Pasker. He served a complete ten-year sentence for armed robbery at Attica in New York. Though he was a model prisoner with no disciplinary record, he was repeatedly denied parole because of his membership in the Skinhead Nation."

Having reached the end of the printout, Jade sat down.

She opened her mouth to ask why everyone was still looking at her when the low growling murmur of Mack's voice came to her ear.

"And what is the Skinhead Nation?"

She had no answer beyond the word 'gang' and perhaps a few adjectives like 'violent,' none of which would be particularly descriptive here. She knew nothing else about Skinheads. Dennis had sent minimal information, because, she suspected, he was pissed-off about his tires. She knew she would have to cover his costs. For a fleeting moment, she thought she might ask Charlie to cover it since he was the responsible party, but he was sitting very still and staring at her, waiting for her answer to Mack's question.

She cleared her throat and forced out a few words. "I'll get right on that."

"I have it here," said Mara. She had been busy at the keyboard, and her printer spewed a full-page summary. "It is from American open sources, not your library, but it may be enough."

She tore the paper off the printer and handed it to her with a smile.

Jade stood again and read the entire thing aloud, doing her best to keep her shaking knees out of her voice. The article covered the cultural aspects, the origins in Britain, and the gang's prevalence in American prisons.

"While some youths who like the music and shave their heads are not white supremacists," she read in summary, "in the US, at least, they have become increasingly associated with neo-nazism. They often have white supremacist tattoos and are known to employ extreme violence."

Having delivered her short lecture to a roomful of the extremely violent—though, one would hope, not neo-Nazis—she considered her duty done and sat down again.

Skosh spoke up.

"Kestutis told me more Americans have arrived in the country with similar tattoos to those on Pasker, especially the 88 that stands for Heil Hitler. They are not popular with the sixteen or seventeen Lithuanians—that count has been fluctuating—who have joined them. There are twenty-four Americans bivouacked at Prion's compound near Nida. Make that twenty-three without Pasker. Speaking of that incident, I need more information about what happened there."

The information would not be forthcoming anytime soon. At that moment, the row of sensor lights next to Mara's computer became multi-colored strobes. Frantic pounding and shouting at the front door of the smaller safehouse brought Jade to her feet, and everybody around her, Skosh included, drew their weapons.

NINETEEN

The man outside shouted, "Jade, Jade, please!" She recognized Rimas's voice as he repeated, "You must help us."

Pound, bang, pound.

"It's an emergency."

Pound, pound.

"You have to be in there. It's too cold to be anywhere else."

Rattle, pound.

"Are you asleep? Wake up!"

Skosh moved toward the rug. Mack whispered, "No," before putting his gun away and taking Jade's arm. He gave a series of hand signals she did not understand to Charlie, who raised his chin in assent. Another signal was directed at Skosh and he holstered his weapon. The others in the room remained poised to fire at the intruder.

Mack led her through the rug. The racket at the door increased. Rimas sounded frantic. Backing against the wall next to the hinges, Mack signaled for Jade to open it. She wanted to argue, desperate to make him let her handle it for Rimas's sake, but she remembered Skosh's uncertainty about the interpreter and contented herself with being glad Mack did not have a weapon in his hand at the moment.

She opened the door. "Rimas, what …?"

That was as far as she got before he burst in shoving something in her face. Not a gun or knife, but a piece of paper, capable of a paper cut, she supposed, but no more than that.

"Jade, Antanas …."

That was as far as he got before he found himself face first against the back of the door, which had been slammed shut by Mack as he drove the full weight of Rimas's body into it.

The paper fluttered to the floor. Jade picked it up and a name caught her eye. She could not help saying it aloud. "Prion?"

It was exactly the wrong thing to say. Sergei and Steve appeared on her side of the rug but were ordered back with a jerk of Mack's head. Fortunately, they made no more noise than a zephyr, and Rimas was still kissing the door, so he could not see them or their guns. With a significant glance and a lift of his chin, Mack ordered Jade to read the paper.

"It's from a court in Michigan, an order telling Antanas Dockus, that's Rimas's brother, that he must vacate his flat by tomorrow. This is in a probate case concerning the estate of Thomas Prion. It has been endorsed and forwarded through a Lithuanian court. I can't read that part. There is a certified translation of the order into Lithuanian."

She paused as it hit her. "Rimas, was Tommy Taurus's real name Prion?"

His voice muffled by the door, Rimas said, "Yes."

Skosh tried to come in. He retreated under Mack's glare.

Mack held Rimas fast while roughly but thoroughly checking him for weapons. When he stepped back, he reminded her again of a big cat watching possible prey, ready to move in any direction.

Rimas turned cautiously, instinctively keeping his hands up, palms out.

"Tell us," said Mack.

Jade caught Rimas's glance. She could see he was full of questions but could not help him with any answers. She asked a question of her own to get him started.

"Did Tommy tell Antanas he was giving him the flat?"

"Yes. We told you...."

Mack interrupted. "Did he give a deed?"

"No," Rimas whispered, defeated. "He just made him promise never to leave it."

"You speak German?"

"No, I..."

Mack looked at Jade as if he were talking to her, giving her a string of instructions, none of which she could decipher, because they were all in German for the benefit of the listeners beyond the rug. She nodded as though she understood. He took her fleece jacket off the door hook and threw it to her, grabbed the paper from her hand, and pushed Rimas through the door as he opened it. She was still trying to put on her jacket when she reached the back seat of Rimas's Škoda. Mack held the door open and climbed in next to her.

As he put the car in gear and pulled out onto the road to the ferry, Rimas said, "Jade, I am thinking this man could either help Antanas or hurt him badly. Am I right?"

She had no answer to give him.

…

Rimas wore a worried scowl. With sideways glances, he studied the man as they climbed three long, straight flights up the elegant staircase in Antanas's building. Jade trailed behind them, puffing a bit. There was no sign of stress or fatigue in the older man who never slowed, never hurried. *Not surprising considering the skill with which he handled me at the door,* thought Rimas.

"Tell me about Thomas," said the man after telling both brothers to call him Mack.

They stood just inside the door of the apartment. There had been no other introductions, no invitation to sit. Antanas fought tears as he recounted the most important romance of his life. Rimas watched Mack for his reaction. His face betrayed nothing of his thoughts.

"His father is Earl Prion? And he disapproved?" asked Mack.

It occurred to Rimas that Mack might also be the sort of father to disapprove of most things—this above all.

"Yes," said Antanas. "He was vicious to Tommy. Hateful. He even threatened his ex-wife and accused her of making Tommy gay just to spite him."

He shifted from one foot to another, evidently having had the same thought about Mack's attitude. "My father also disapproved. Our fathers' disapproval was one of the things that bonded us. Tommy left shortly after his mother's funeral and said he would be back, but then he became ill and …"

"He contracted AIDS in the United States?"

Was Mack's minimally raised eyebrow a comment or just part of the question?

"Yes. It took him quickly." Antanas hurried to explain. "We were neither of us exclusive; we just loved each other. He said he would be back and would explain about the flat and other things."

"Other things? What things?"

Antanas shrugged.

Mack's blue eyes scanned the graceful tall windows to the polished parquet floor and the magnificent drum set near the wall across from where they stood.

"Tell me what he said when he said goodbye—the exact words."

This startled Antanas enough to arrest his tears for the moment.

"He… He told me not to leave the flat."

"The words. I want the words."

It was an unmistakable command. Antanas took a deep breath and closed his eyes.

"Our future is here, Antanas. Do not leave the flat. I will explain everything when I come back."

The tears began again.

"Where were his eyes when he said this?" Mack's peremptory tone held no sign of contempt but was equally devoid of compassion.

Antanas tilted his head and wrinkled his brow. He did not understand.

"What was he seeing?" Mack was losing patience, his voice becoming ever sharper.

Shrugging with a slight shake of his head at this madman, Antanas swept a gracile hand toward the drums. "There!"

Rimas exchanged bewildered glances with Jade and his brother as Mack inspected the drum set and the floor around it. He lifted a stand that held a cymbal and shifted two other pieces, including the large bass drum. Rimas shook his head, warning Antanas to quell a growing protest.

Mack drew a knife that was too large to be carried as a mere useful tool. He knelt on the floor and pried three strips of the intricate parquet wood out of their places side by side, then reached into the subsequent hole and pulled out a plastic folder tied with string. It contained a thick stack of folded documents.

The sight of the gun under his coat, as Mack slid this find into an inner pocket, added more confirmation of what Rimas had suspected when he stood immobilized with his nose against the door of Jade's little house. She gave him an unnecessary look of wide-eyed warning. He knew exactly what he was dealing with.

Mack took Jade's arm and led her toward the door, where he turned to Rimas

"Do you fight?"

Rimas nodded.No use to deny it.

"Your brother will need protection," said Mack. "Hide him somewhere. Not here. Lock this door, close the curtains, and leave. Now."

"If there is danger," said Rimas, "let me take Jade to safety with us."

Mack gazed at him for several seconds before nodding in assent without consulting Jade. Rimas realized the man had been making a calculated decision about his character.

He and his brother followed them through the downstairs door and out into a cold blast from the Baltic.

"If he values his life," Mack said quietly, though loud enough for Rimas to hear, "Skosh has followed my directions and is waiting outside."

Rimas spotted the car a few meters down the street, recognizing in the driver's seat the American who had been working with Kestutis. Next to him sat a brown-haired man he had not seen before, but he was familiar with the air of strictly business with which the man scanned the street, front, back, and side to side.

He took Jade's arm from Mack and led her and Antanas to the Škoda to drive them into hiding. From what or whom, he was not sure, but avoiding the proximity of this Mack character would be a healthy start. If it could be done.

TWENTY

Skosh drove to the ferry in an uncomfortable silence. It bothered him that Jade was not with them. He had to ask the question but knew no answer would be satisfactory.

"Why is Jade not coming with us?"

Mack answered from the back seat with a question.

"The young man she calls Rimas, why did he come to her for help?"

"Maybe he remembered how she handled the landlord when you needed the safehouse two days early, and so he figured she might be able to help with his problem."

Skosh did not disguise the touch of resentment in his words.

"Why did he know how she handled the landlord?"

"He was her interpreter that night."

"Interpreter," Mack said in a flat tone. "Because she does not speak Lithuanian. Nor Russian. Nor German."

These were statements, not questions, with Mack's voice becoming smoother as he delivered each phrase. "Where did you get this 'interpreter?'"

Skosh distinctly heard the quotation marks. He took a breath.

"Kestutis provided him. You approved Kestutis."

The car boarded the ferry with its occupants in perfect silence, a silence broken by Mack when the boat set off for the other shore.

"I have other information about Kestutis and for one purpose, only for that purpose, is his involvement acceptable. I approved him to help you coordinate with the local authorities. Not to know where my safehouse is. Not to introduce an unknown interpreter into the operation. Not to further complicate your egregious mistake of trying to salvage something that may be without remedy."

The man did not shout, but each 'not' contained a special emphasis that made Skosh cringe inwardly with every iteration. The only saving grace about this dressing down was that the car made it inconvenient for Mack to punctuate his anger with fists.

Skosh said nothing. Mack continued.

"Your authorities signed an agreement to give me access to information I need. You know very well that I do not care which of your political groups is out of favor or which politicians are compromised. I know these things already. What little is left of such things that I do not know, I can find in The New York Times. What I need is information on the killers, madmen, criminals, assassins, and double agents that you pay me to fight for you. I need that information to stay alive. Instead of abiding by the contract agreed to by your organization, you chose to protect your precious vault and by doing so, you put Kestutis's man, a man I know nothing about, at my safehouse, and now that man has seen me."

Skosh laid his forehead on his knuckles at the top of the steering wheel as the ferry chugged along. "Kestutis vouched ..."

"Kestutis is the son and grandson of anti-Soviet partisans who fought in the forests after the war. He is a fighter. Not all of the original fighters were sound. Some began their careers aiding the Nazis. War creates ambiguity in the characters of men. This man also is a fighter. I do not know his origins, and he has seen me and my safehouse."

At this, Steve turned around and made eye contact with Mack, watching for a signal.

Skosh sat up. "You can't know that." Both belligerence and defeat inflected his voice at the same time.

"I do know it. I handled him. He recognized what I am and made a decision, a conscious decision not to react. We knew each other. Charlemagne is vastly outnumbered, and you have made it infinitely worse by bringing with you a woman whose presence has no purpose but to keep me ignorant of the enemies we must face within the next thirty hours or sooner."

As the ferry docked, Skosh put the car in gear. They drove in palpable tension down an empty road with a thick evergreen forest arching overhead like a tunnel. The tension heightened as they pulled up behind the team's safehouse, where the blackness of thick forest formed a wall and where Skosh expected to be more vulnerable than ever to Mack's fists.

But as Mack shoved him through the back door of the team's house, he said, "I remind you, Skosh, you worry about your secrets and your career when it is your life that is at stake."

TWENTY-ONE

"Rimas, where are we going?"

He glanced at his passenger. She was indeed pretty. And he loved her accent. He had learned British English and enjoyed cataloging the differences every time she spoke. She was so very American, supremely exotic.

Antanas answered her from the back seat.

"We are going to Užupis. It is a special place. Have you been to Paris?"

"Yes. I attended the Sorbonne. Do you speak French?"

Rimas heard a hopeful note in her voice.

"No," said Antanas. "Do you know a place called Montmartre, where there are artists?"

"Yes. I lived not far from there."

"Užupis is the Montmartre of Lithuania. You will like it. I have a friend who paints. It is very Bohemian and original in Užupis. There is no plumbing even, and some houses have no roof or windows, but it is full of interesting people. I know one who has the perfect motto. 'Never fight. Never win. Never surrender.'"

"Is it far?"

"About three hours," said Rimas as he accelerated the car. "But we will make rather better time than that. I know someone who has done it in two hours, nine minutes."

"What? No! I can't be gone that long. Stop. Take me back, please, Rimas. It's important. I must go back."

She was searching for her door handle. He took hold of her arm, his left hand remaining on the wheel, his foot pressed onto the accelerator. The odometer needle read 160 kilometers per hour. She squirmed under his grasp, trying and failing to pry his fingers open.

Antanas spoke from the back with a voice full of surprise.

"Your friend agreed that you should come as well, for your safety. Don't worry. I will find space for both of us."

"My friend! He is not a friend. He …" She interrupted herself with a note of despair.

"If he is not a friend," said Rimas, "what is he? An enemy?"

"No."

Her voice had become small, her manner calm. She stopped reaching for the door handle, and Rimas let go.

"Not a friend and not an enemy," he said quietly. "What was his name again?"

He could tell she knew his purpose in asking. She thought before answering.

"Not 'again', Rimas. I have no doubt you remember very well that he told you other people call him Mack. If fishing for information I don't have is your reason for taking me away, then you can turn around now. I know nothing else. This is a game of grandmaster chess, and I am nothing more than a beginner, at best a pawn. Please. Take me back."

"You will like my friends, Jade," Antanas said in a pleading voice. "Vilnius is a beautiful old city. You must see it."

...

How she would have loved to go there as a tourist, to revel in history and culture and art, to meet exciting new people. She corrected the thought. Interesting people. Exciting had become overrated. Jade longed to sip wine and listen to music. She wanted lively conversation on inconsequential topics. She badly needed a bath.

She glanced at Rimas at the wheel next to her and noticed for the first time, the hard set of his jaw. There was more to him than she had realized. He did not fit the motto of Užupis. He would fight, she decided, and he would win.

"I don't have any clothes with me," she said. "Not even a toothbrush, or a hairbrush."

It was the missing hairbrush that threatened to bring tears. She knew how to stop them, would normally stop them. Jade was adept at controlling her emotions, but maybe this time she could weaponize them. Rimas had turned out to be tougher than she originally thought. This newly discovered hard edge suggested he did not find Mack as alien to him as she did. But he was a young man and had never mentioned a sister who would have hardened him to feminine manipulation. He might be susceptible.

She released the flood.

…

Rimas pulled over at Antanas's insistence. Luckily, his brother had a clean handkerchief and soothing words. The handkerchief was soon soaked, and the sweet words initially sparked only a pitiable wailing, but eventually, Antanas was able to elicit a few intelligible sentences.

"I can't… I don't have any makeup with me. I look a fright. These are old clothes, rags. I can't… I just can't meet new people like this. Please don't make me. Please, Rimas, please take me back!"

Rimas told himself his decision did not amount to capitulation. It was more of a reevaluation. Yes, that was it, he decided. It had nothing to do with his sudden inability to deal with the hysterical female sitting next to him. There would be other ways to get the information out of her if she had any. This display made him think that was un-likely.

"Listen!" he shouted over the din.

Jade subsided into shudders.

"We are almost at Užupis. We will see Antanas settled safely. After that—no more than half an hour, I promise—I have decided I will take you back."

The shuddering ceased, and Rimas refrained from adding the words, 'but not to Mack.'

He had someone else in mind.

TWENTY-TWO

Mack handed Mara the packet of documents he had taken from the apartment and ac-companied it with a fast, insistent series of instruc-tions in German. Skosh heard the ominous name, Justin, and tensed. Mara took the packet apart and fed page after page into the fax machine.

As Skosh fell asleep on his folded arms at the kitchen table, the voices on the other side of the rug melted into disjointed dreams. There were dis-cussions, between Mack and Charlie, Charlie and everybody, Mara and Sergei, and then more order barking by Mack. Then Candace had her say, grey eyes flashing vengeance, while his boss's boss,

Henry, reinforced the new directive about information security breaches.

Henry growled. No, that was Mack, Skosh decided through the haze of a half-doze. Maybe roaring would be a better word. There was a name, a contact he had never heard of. An in-country contact, who duly received a call from Mack on the telephone in Skosh's kitchen with instructions about the street Antanas lived on. The team's phone was tied up with the faxing of those documents.

Skosh sank into a deeper sleep. There must have been a quiet period for the team as well, he thought, as he woke late in the afternoon with a sore neck and an extreme caffeine-withdrawal headache. He went through the rug in search of coffee and filled a cup at the team's machine.

Nearby, next to Mara's computer, sat the console of blinking, many-colored lights from Sergei's myriad perimeter sensors. Mack stood before it, wearing an earbud. Its wire led to a small receiver on his belt.

The room, the entire two houses, felt dark and cold as everybody sat wearing earbuds, sipping coffee, and saying nothing, with only Mack and Skosh standing. The phone next to the computer rang. Mack moved like a cat to answer it. Skosh congratulated himself on what he thought was a pretty good job of not letting on that the sudden jangle had stabbed his brain. The coffee would cure it in time.

Mack hung up the phone, turned on his transmitter, and began a long series of statements or instructions in the microphone on his wire. He grabbed his coat and pushed Skosh through the rug, handed him his jacket, and led him out onto the street.

Skosh assumed the one-sided conversation Mack was holding via the wire was directed toward the team. The man communicated with him only by means of glares and impatient gestures.

Hurry up. Put your coat on. Stand here. Don't talk.

He said all of this without speaking. Skosh watched him inspect his rental car with a small flashlight. It must be Sergei on the other end of the conversation, he thought, telling Mack what to look for in the way of Skosh's private alarms. It was the exponential creep factor of knowing the light-eyed Russian held that kind of information that bothered him most. Eventually satisfied it was free of booby traps, Mack unlocked the driver's door and indicated he should get in.

The talking in Mack's ear did not allow conversation until they were almost on the ferry.

As Skosh had expected, they secured the car several blocks away from Antanas's flat and made their way to it carefully. Mack took a signal from a watcher across the street, and they entered the building.

They made no noise, but Skosh doubted they would have been heard anyway over the din coming from the upstairs apartment. Mack gently tried the door. It was locked. He pulled out a lock-picking tool and opened it.

They walked into an interrogation. Rimas stood against the wall on Skosh's right with his head back, holding a bloody rag to his nose. A drum set had been scattered around the room. Most of the pieces were bent or broken.

Kestutis interrupted an angry monologue directed at Rimas to emphasize his point by slapping Jade, who sat on the floor with her back against a badly damaged bass drum.

Skosh could see this was not the first slap she had received. Her cheekbones were bruised, and one eye was rimmed in purple. Her upper lip had a cut on one side and the lower was swollen. The sight pushed him closer to crossing the line between babysitter and specialist. He wanted to kill Kestutis at that moment and knew he would have if Mack had not given him a warning glance when he raised his hand toward his holster.

The entire edifice of Skosh's previously stoic character was falling like a house of cards.

TWENTY-THREE

When the man hit her a third time, Jade reconsidered her early desire for a little bit of danger. This had now, officially, crossed the line from little bit to some and was well on the way to too much. She was sure a front tooth had loosened. Her nose did not bleed all over her clothes like Rimas's, but it was only a matter of time and the location of the next blow.

The man who wanted to know about Mack was about the same age, blond with a hint of grey like Mack's, and violent like him, too. When the man met them at Antanas's flat, Rimas had initially treated him as a trusted friend and called him Kestutis.

That bonhomie ended when the man broke Rimas's nose demanding answers to such questions as where was Antanas and where were the documents that had been discovered under the drums. Besides punching each question into Rimas's body, Kestutis illustrated his intent by destroying most of the drum set and strewing the pieces across the room.

Jade's interrogation resumed, but by then Rimas had provided an example of total silence that she followed. If he found his friend untrustworthy—and she supposed a broken nose could sour any friendship—then Jade was not about to divulge anything she knew, which was precious little anyway. Thus, the repeated bruising slaps across her face.

What with clanging cymbals thrown against walls and drums being kicked in, not to mention shouting and scuffling, she wondered what Antanas's neighbors must be thinking and why they did nothing. She had fallen with her back against what had once been the large bass drum when she saw the door open. She hoped it meant police. It did not.

It was Mack.

His presence did not comfort her, but that Skosh stood to his right made her heart leap.

Kestutis turned to the intruders and dropped the hand he had raised to hit her again.

"Who in hell are you now?" he said to Mack, using English.

"Most still call me Mack. We have come to retrieve the girl." His voice had that low, even growl she had come to know and fear.

"Are you her lover? Is that why you are here? More likely you are her father." Kestutis spat the words, heavy with sarcasm.

"That is not your question, my friend. What you need to know is whether I am willing to die for her." Mack paused in his still, slow way. "I am not." He pointed to Skosh. "But he is."

"Pfft! He is an office boy."

Mack's next pause lasted half a beat longer before he answered, in an unconcerned, almost bored, soft voice.

"I know that he is at least as capable as your man there." He pointed to Rimas still holding a rag to his nose.

"What were the papers you took from here?" Kestutis demanded. Then, without waiting for an answer, he took a step forward and pointing his chin at Skosh, said, "If he can fight as you say, we are evenly matched. I want those papers."

Mack held up a hand to halt him.

"I think not unless one of you is also willing to die for the girl. Our sole purpose here is to retrieve her."

Mack stepped to one side of the door and breathed normally, but she sensed his tension. He never took his eyes off his opponent.

"You cannot recover the papers," he said. "I have secured them. You may leave." He indicated the door with a minimal lift of his chin.

After a brief mutual glare, Kestutis made up his mind. "We will meet soon."

"I look forward to it."

The man moved almost as silently down the stairs as Mack had done coming up, leaving a sense of unfinished business behind him.

Having stopped the bleeding from his nose, Rimas stood awkwardly shuffling his feet.

Jade wished fervently that Kestutis and Mack had beat each other to a pulp for what they had done to her but knew better than to expect it. She held no more than a nanosecond of their consideration. She also seriously doubted Skosh would be willing to die for her.

Mack held Rimas in his characteristic scary-as-hell blue-eyed glare. It surprised her, then, when Rimas broke the silence not with belligerence, perhaps, but at least irritation.

"Why did you let me take her?"

"That is my affair."

"Who are you and why is she with you?"

"I have given you and Kestutis a name. Is he your mentor? Did he train you to fight?"

Rimas paused, considering, as the purple bruising spread beneath and around his eyes, highlighted by the surrounding fair skin.

"He has been good to me," he said finally. "I owe him everything."

Mack raised one eyebrow. "But not your brother's life?"

Rimas had no answer. Silence reigned again until he seemed to come to a decision.

"I wanted Jade to tell me who you are," he said, looking Mack in the eye. "But she had hysterics, a fit I have never seen before. I did not know what to do. I brought her back and called Kestutis to help me."

Jade allowed herself a small self-satisfied smile until she saw that both Mack and Skosh had noticed it. She would not be able to use that ploy with either of them. But then, she imagined both had enough experience to be proof against it anyway.

Skosh gave Rimas a scornful smile.

"And he fucking hit you when you tried to defend her? Some mentor."

Jade remembered the bruises on Skosh after one of his interviews with Mack but considered that theirs was no mentor/protégé relationship.

Rimas answered quickly. "No, I asked for help with an interrogation, and he was giving it, but I had to tell him about this man, Mack, that I had met at your house because that was the intelligence I wanted from her."

Skosh winced, and Rimas continued.

"He wanted to know more, but I could not tell him about my brother's problem. Kestutis has no use for Antanas."

Rimas looked at Mack. "He asked about you and how you found the documents. He said the words 'your brother's documents'. Did you tell him about the papers you found?"

"You know I did not."

Rimas sighed. "I would not tell him, and he became furious. He broke my nose and then went back to Jade to try for the information he wanted. She said nothing and I was debating what to do when you came in. I was sure she was about to suffer more than a broken nose."

Jade picked herself up off the floor, shaking not a little, but whole and intact and grateful that her nose remained centered on her face.

Rimas held up his hands in a pleading gesture.

"Kestutis is a good man, a patriot, and a hero, but he is not himself. He is convinced Prion is doing something good for Lithuania."

Mack let the silence build for a moment before he broke it.

"But you are not."

Rimas nudged a cymbal on the floor with the toe of his boot, then raised his eyes to him. "How does killing a gentle Lithuanian help my country?"

"Did he come to kill Antanas or was he looking for the papers?"

"Both, I think. He was angry that I had moved my brother and wanted me to tell him where. Thank you for advising it. He is safe."

"And Prion? Is he doing something good for Lithuania?"

"Tommy told my brother that his father hated Lithuania after his wife left him and Tommy admitted he was gay. I tried to explain this to Kestutis, but he would not listen."

Rimas turned to Skosh with a pleading look. "He is a good man, Skosh. Give him time; give me time to get him away from Prion."

Jade marveled that Rimas had grasped so much of the truth but mistook Skosh for the boss here. It was the man standing next to him who was calling the shots. Skosh threw a significant glance to his left.

Rimas nodded his understanding and offered Mack information in return for his friend's life. A move Jade hoped she would never have to make.

"Something has happened to Prion's money," he told Mack. "He will try to act earlier than planned."

TWENTY-FOUR

They stamped their feet and swung their arms to keep circulation going. Misha did not wear a scarf. Michael's was failing in its mission to keep his face warm. The briefing his father gave him about the late afternoon's events caused clouds of breath in the air and of doom in Michael's mind.

"You may want to consider this man Rimas," said Misha.

Michael raised an eyebrow and he continued.

"Twice now he has declined to fight."

"Is he shy?"

"No. He is disciplined. He took an undeserved beating from his teacher without replying. That is not shyness. Like you, he knows sometimes not entering a contest is wiser than winning it." Misha paused and said, "I should not have taken this commission. I am sorry."

A compliment and an apology on the same day, Michael thought. But he could not let the apology stand.

"We made the decision together, Papa. Access to their information was too important to turn it down."

"That bank is east of Berlin. I heard you asking Sergei who he thinks may still be assigned in that area. Are you thinking the SVR is involved?"

"I am. I sense another mind behind Prion, not just money. This man Rimas, what makes you think he would be willing to join us?"

Misha turned to look at him. "He was born to fight."

"How can you know?"

"I know his teacher."

"Kestutis? He is deceived by Prion."

"His judgment has deserted him, not his skill."

They walked further along the shore of the lagoon in silence, while Michael considered his next question. Most of the changes he had seen in his father lately seemed positive, but any change at all felt threatening until he forced himself to view the man through adult eyes.

"Papa, if Kestutis has lost his judgment, he may be mistaken about Rimas."

"He has been deceived, Michael, but not by Rimas. You should embrace this deception as additional weight for your suspicion that there is another player. Prion does not have the capacity for a deep game. Regardless of his present deception, Kestutis could always spot talent. He would not have taken on this young man without it."

"Has he killed?"

"Rimas?"

"Yes."

"I doubt it."

"Then what can we offer him? I don't want anyone motivated solely by money. Protection from our enemies binds us more securely. He is too young to have serious enemies, especially if he has not killed. Why would he volunteer for such a life?"

Misha stopped and turned to him with a sardonic smile.

"You can offer protection for those who are important to him."

"Who?"

"His brother. Also, he will want to see that Kestutis is undeceived and alive. And there is the woman."

"Which woman?"

Misha's brow furrowed, forcing Michael to think along an unfamiliar path.

"Jade? But Skosh wants...."

Misha sighed audibly, a sound meant to remind him of the odds against them. Michael could be more ruthless than his father—if that were possible—but occasionally he caught himself wishing for another world in which there were no losses.

"I will need to test him," he said.

"Of course."

"And she may not...."

"Leave that to me."

TWENTY-FIVE

Jade gave herself a much-needed sponge bath, remaining vigilant behind the supposedly locked bathroom door and thankfully, she was uninterrupted. They had met pandemonium when they returned from Klaipeda, with free-flowing f-words from Skosh as he helped the team prepare—for what, she didn't know and didn't care. The bruises on her face occupied most of her attention. Surely they would fade in time, wouldn't they?

Rimas's nose was still crooked. Skosh had fitted him with an earbud and transmitter because he was to accompany Charlie that night. Unarmed. He would be the only unarmed person in the group.

His introduction to the team had been entertaining. Steve was less than friendly, but nowhere near as unfriendly as Sergei when Rimas's eyes latched onto Mara. Rimas understood every Russian threat Sergei threw at him and responded in kind. Jade could see him wondering if he had joined the wrong side.

Charlie cooled the situation as only his ice-cold manner could.

"Rimas will stay by me on the Baltic side of the compound to translate anything we may hear. He will never go near Mara, Sergei, and now he knows better than to even look at her."

He issued more orders and instructions, and Jade heard a few dark jokes at Rimas's expense, spoken in English so that he fully understood before the team had finally slunk out of the house.

Their absence made Jade feel safe enough to use the bathroom.

She unpacked a worn pair of corduroys and a flannel shirt sporting old paint splotches from past decorating projects. She had brought them just in case she would be required to march in the rain or dig a ditch. They were the last clean clothes in her suitcase and the occasion qualified as ditch digging.

While she detangled and tied up her hair in a tight ponytail, she laughed into the mirror at the Jade of yesterday, who thought of make-up as a necessity. The smile hurt but made the bruises less ugly.

Cautiously opening the door and listening carefully, she crept the few steps into the empty little kitchen. A single bare lightbulb hanging from a wire over the table gave her enough light to see that she was alone. At first, she sighed with relief, but the silence had a creepy quality after all the noise and threats and incomprehensible language, even words supposedly spoken in English. If this were a movie, she thought, the eerie music would be playing, and the stupid heroine would proceed to investigate those dark corners against all common sense.

Leaving the dark corners and hanging rug alone, she sat down at her laptop like a good girl, found Charlie's new list of questions, lengthy because of the hours she had been gone, and got to work.

She called Dennis to give him a heads-up before she tied up the phone line by hitting send. He was still pretty grumpy about his tires and not all that gracious about her pledge to make it up to him. A fresh pot of hot coffee cheered her up until she turned from pouring a mug and sloshed a sizable splotch on the floor, because Mack was sitting at the table, across from her chair. He had an earbud in his ear and held a portable radio.

She could not have had her back turned for more than a few seconds. A pin dropping to the floor would have made a noise like a gong in that silent, close space. Her voice came through for her after a few stammers.

"Would you like a cup of coffee?"

He nodded with a half-smile.

She sat across from him, holding her cup with both hands, wondering what he would say or do next and dreading it. He had let Rimas take her to Vilnius, she was sure, to force Skosh into giving up access to the vault's computer. Without Jade, there would be no Dennis to make her system work. Skosh could never convince the assistant to carry on without her.

Knowing why he sent her away, though, did not explain why Mack then arranged her rescue. She was sure it was a rescue. It had all the earmarks of danger and pain and bruising followed by intervention by a scary guy telling the other scary guy to let her go. And the quiet, minimal way in which he did it, without any actual violence, though she had sensed his readiness to fight, was an engineering job of the most subtle kind.

Her internal question remained, why had he done it? His insistence that he would not die for her held more truth in her mind than the fact that he risked a fight to retrieve her.

She looked up from her coffee to find him regarding her silently. The alien blue eyes again reminded her that she would never understand this man. He broke the silence.

"Sometimes, the most unlikely events bring forth the best intelligence."

Jade did not hide her bewilderment.

"Kestutis has become Prion's man. Your brief captivity gave us enough intelligence to solve half the puzzle."

He took a sip from his mug and continued, answering her unspoken question.

"You required rescue when I needed information. It was convenient. Also, I cannot allow Skosh to have more reasons to reproach himself. Please do not make the mistake of thinking I will make a habit of protecting you."

If he was in the mood to answer unvoiced questions, maybe a direct one, out loud, would succeed.

"Are you going to kill me?" she asked.

He answered with a sardonic smile. "No."

"Are you going to kill Skosh?"

She shivered and gulped air when he did not answer.

"What can I give you that will stop that? I mean, aside from my password, but anything else. Anything. Name it."

Jade had reserved the password for purposes of future negotiation, but she meant that she was offering anything in the way of information, of course, so she could not hide her alarm when the man smiled at her in that way. The smile widened further when her wide eyes betrayed shock.

"You must be more careful what you put on the table, Jade. In all of our contracts, it is my interpretation of the terms that controls."

The following two-hour grilling by Mack covered every unimportant detail of her job and left Jade feeling safe again after her unthinking offer. He wasn't taking her up on it, so she began to relax.

Then he stood over her, offering his hand to help her up. She automatically took it, feeling the power with which he boosted her to her feet.

"Come," he said and began leading her back toward the bedroom.

She tried to pull away.

"I… I didn't mean… I was referring to information."

He gave a soft, amused chuckle, but held her arm as he led, or pulled, her through the bedroom door.

"By now, Kestutis has told Prion about you. I cannot leave you alone and you need sleep, proper sleep, on a bed. I have set the perimeter sensors to give the alarm on the radio." He held up the portable in his other hand. "Now, lie down."

Jade had no idea how she would be able to sleep with this man in the same room, let alone sitting next to her on the bed, propped up by several pillows. She lay flat out, her shoulders raised slightly on just two pillows, her body stiff with fright and her eyes wide open. Mack quietly put an arm around her shoulders, barely touching her flannel shirt. She felt relaxed by this, almost against her will, and turned on her side automatically so that she curled up facing him. Her last thought before exhaustion overtook all thought was that no man, including the father who had shown up on rare occasions when she was a girl, ever made her feel so protected as this man did, this man who had insisted he would not die for her.

TWENTY-SIX

"Do you prefer Rimantas or Rimas?" asked Charlie from the back seat.

"Really, Charlie?" said Skosh as he turned the car toward Nida. "Are you trying to tell him he has a choice about what you guys call him?"

Rimas looked over his shoulder at Charlie. They were barely acquainted and came from different countries, but they shared a fighting culture. He suspected Skosh might fight as well. He had the muscle development and the usual, mildly belligerent attitude of latent violence, but he acted like he played only a side role. This much, Rimas understood. He also sensed that in the next few hours, Charlie would become either a valuable ally or an enemy.

Everything else about these people remained a mystery. And one was Russian.

"Call me Rimas," he said

Skosh cut the headlights and coasted to a stop under an evergreen canopy tucked into a dark stand of trees hidden from the road. "The compound is straight ahead. We're facing south." He switched on the transmitter attached to his belt. "I'll monitor you guys from here."

"Like hell you will," said Charlie. "You'll come with us."

"It's not good for me to get too close."

"Spare me your babysitter rules. You'll come with us and protect Rimas. He's not armed."

Both Skosh and Rimas turned around in their seats. "I can't …"

Charlie interrupted. "Don't make the mistake of thinking I'm as patient as my father, Skosh."

"He should not come inside with me, Charlie," said Rimas. "He looks too exotic. It will raise questions. I will ask them if they have seen Kestutis and a few other questions, casually, while I place your listening device."

Inside the long wooden building that housed Prion's Lithuanian volunteers, Rimas recognized a former childhood classmate and three others he had trained with as a teenager. It felt good to enjoy a bottle of beer amidst Lithuanian voices. He followed Charlie's advice and avoided showing too much curiosity about Prion.

"I'm looking for Kestutis," he said. "I thought I might find him here."

"No, he's not sure about Prion yet," said Vytautas scornfully. "He went to Šiauliai to look for something, probably information."

"To look for something or somebody," interrupted Feliksas.

Rimas sipped his beer and wondered if he looked as dangerous as these two. Feliksas had added muscle mass since they were teenagers but seemed more confident and sober. Vytautas had the same wild-eyed look, though, the same jumpiness, and Rimas remembered he could never be trusted in a fight.

"You should join us," said Vytautas as he opened another beer.

"I don't know…."

"It's a chance to kill some Russians."

Feliksas hissed at Vytautas. "Don't talk about it. Leave that to Kestutis."

"I'll talk all I want. Rimas is all right."

Another man Rimas did not know sat down on a footlocker next to Vytautas and took away his beer. Feliksas introduced him as being one of those in charge. The man's scrutiny was enough to make Rimas ask no more questions. He finished the beer in his hand and took his leave.

As he slipped through a break in the fence, he expected to meet Charlie at the side of the pathway they had made on their way in. Instead, Sergei whispered to him in Russian from behind a particularly stout pine. Even in mottled moonlight, he recognized the pale grey eyes behind Sergei's balaclava.

"Wear this," he said, handing Rimas an earbud and transmitter. Charlie's voice came over the wire.

"Change of plan. You'll help Sergei place the rest of the touches in Prion's office. Did you find Kestutis?"

Surrounded by forest, instinct made him tilt his head in a minimal, silent negative.

"You have a microphone, Rimas. Just whisper."

"He is in Šiauliai."

"Good. We'll debrief later. Follow Sergei's direction."

Sergei handed him a stick of camo paint and a black balaclava and turned his back to him to lead the way.

The two hesitations came simultaneously, each man noticing the other's momentary pause before they made their silent way back to the hole in the fence.

...

Jade sat up, alarmed, but still next to Mack as the overhead light flooded the bedroom. His arm remained protectively around her shoulders, and he wore a self-satisfied smile. Three men had burst into the room, their hair disheveled, their eyes and hands blackened by night camo paint.

She recognized Skosh and Rimas immediately by their height and belligerence, one by his black hair, the other by his blue eyes. The third, the blond, had to be Charlie.

Skosh opened his mouth to say something. Rimas stepped forward. Mack gathered her into his arms and kissed her every bit as seriously as Skosh had done, but he had the decency to keep his eyes closed like he meant it. She checked.

He let go when the sounds of a brief scuffle had quieted. Jade saw Rimas sitting on the floor against the dresser, once again holding his nose, and Skosh doubled over against a wall. Charlie stood over them looking disgusted.

"All right, Papa. You made your point."

"Which point is that, Michael?" Mack still held Jade with one arm.

"That you are not past it," said Charlie or was his name Michael? Jade suspected she had landed in some family tiff.

"What else?" said Mack in that soft purr.

"That Alex has not entirely succeeded in taming you."

"And?"

Charlie sighed and rolled his eyes.

"That you are correct. They both want the woman. I now agree with your plan. Are you done?"

"Yes."

Mack stood, pushed Skosh up against the wall, and said, "You have three hours to debrief your assistant and sleep. I will instruct Sergei to turn off his devices."

Returning Rimas's glare as he walked to the door, he said, "He will not touch her. This is no time for such nonsense."

What Mack did not do was look at her again. Not even a glance. She felt a little miffed. It had been an excellent kiss.

TWENTY-SEVEN

Skosh locked the door behind them when Rimas, Charlie, and Mack left the room—a symbolic gesture really—and kicked off his shoes. He lay down beside Jade on the bed.

That was as sexy as they were ever going to get, Skosh mused with a sense of loss. They had been told to sleep in order, he knew, to keep them out of the team's meeting. That Rimas would be in that meeting rankled. He had not been armed when he went out with Charlie, but the uneasy combination of suspicion and respect with which the team treated him told Skosh the younger guy was no babysitter. Hell, he might even be under consideration for a job. A deadly one, no doubt.

Once again, he and Jade lay side by side fully dressed on top of the duvet. He quizzed her over every word said during her night with Mack. When she told him of Mack's silence after her question about his own danger, he said nothing for a long enough time that she nudged him, probably thinking he had fallen asleep. He turned his head to look at her, still thinking.

Then she told him about her offer and Mack's smile.

"I don't think I've ever seen him smile," said Skosh. He was sinking into a comfortable lassitude he did not want to leave. Death seemed not so bad in this state.

"He looked younger then, even younger than Charlie," said Jade.

"He's right, you know. All agreements we have with them contain a clause that gives him the right to construe the intention of the parties. He might not need to kill me; he could probably win his point in court and make us print out every word stored in your system."

"Which court would he sue in?" She sounded genuinely curious.

Skosh turned his head and looked at her. "I was being facetious."

"Oh." She paused. "Skosh?"

He raised his eyebrows and waited.

"Who is Alex?"

"His wife."

"He has a wife?"

"He told you they're all married now. Not that they all view being married in the same way as most people. I would have thought Mack did, though."

"I don't think he meant it, Skosh. It's hard to explain. He meant the kiss, but not as a prelude to anything else. He had some other purpose."

"Mack always has multiple agendas."

As far as Skosh was concerned, that kiss was a prelude to something, the son of a bitch. He ground his teeth, comfort gone, and changed the subject.

"He didn't demand your password?"

"No. He just asked questions."

"What questions?"

"He asked about people in the building and especially in the leadership, but none of them operatives, only support staff like me."

"What did he want to know?"

"Nothing secret or even confidential. He didn't even ask for addresses or phone numbers. Mostly, he wanted me to talk about their personalities and any gossip about them or stories they put out about others, no matter how absurd."

After a long silence, she nudged him again. His eyes were still open.

"The bastard," he whispered. Then after a deep breath, "Listen, Jade. When we went out again tonight, I was sure Mack would stay back to protect the safehouse now that it's blown, and I was right. He's been letting Charlie make more and more decisions anyway. In a few hours, he'll talk to you again. I want you to tell him something from me. It's important.

"Tell him not to let his natural inclination to eliminate a supposed threat cloud his judgment. Tell him that. He's wrong. It's not what he thinks. It is not a betrayal, just pressure, purely personal, not operational. Candace is not a threat to anybody but me."

Before he let himself sleep, he made an effort to warn her about the larger threat.

"Whatever you do, talk to me before you agree to anything Mack says. Promise me that, Jade. He's a master at manipulation besides being just fucking dangerous."

Skosh fell asleep before she could answer but woke in what seemed no more than a minute when he felt the presence of Charlie in the open doorway.

"Is there any fucking lock that can stop one of you?" he demanded, springing to a stand.

Charlie's answer was the very image of Mack's smile after that kiss. Skosh was having difficulty forgetting it.

"Get moving," said Charlie. "Now that we have a touch on that hovel where Prion is hosting his banker, I want more information on him. That reminds me...."

He half turned to Jade, who had been trying to sneak past him.

"Your information is slow and incomplete."

Poking her sternum with a forefinger, he continued, "Stop playing games, Jade. You can skip the encryption if that is what's taking so long. We've known the key for some time, and you confirmed it this morning. Don't look so surprised. Your assistant had it bookmarked on his bedside table. Sidney Reilly he is not. I've left a list of questions on the table by your notebook. Get to work."

"That's ludicrous, Charlie," said Jade with a defiant glare. "The material is still classified. Just because you're cleared to see it does not mean I can broadcast it to the world by sending it unprotected across seven time zones."

He answered her with a head-to-toe examination, stopping at important points. "You have fifteen minutes to make yourself ..." Another smiling pause, then, "Presentable."

Skosh spoke through his teeth. "That's enough, Charlie."

"Unclench your fists, Skosh. Her ultimate fate is your responsibility, but you know you won't affect it that way."

TWENTY-EIGHT

It was a working breakfast with food that, though made by Lithuanians, tasted foreign to Rimas. These were all foreigners, and one was even a filthy Russian—the worst kind of Russian. He might as well have had 'checkist' tattooed to his forehead, he was so obviously KGB.

Rimas worried again that he had it all wrong, that Kestutis was right and he deserved his broken nose. Then he remembered Antanas. Mack had been correct about the danger. Kestutis had been sent to kill his brother, and the filthy Russian had fixed and bandaged his nose. It hurt like hell, but it was straight again, though the Russian's nose remained crooked.

Sergei was a typical fucking dictatorial know-it-all Russian, though.

Rimas spotted Jade as she came through the rug with Skosh. He gazed at her bruised face. A new resentment rose in his mind concerning that kiss. What did Mack think he was doing? Kestutis was right. He was old enough to be her father. Was there something going on there? She was younger than Charlie for fuck's sake.

Rimas's English vocabulary had expanded in just a few hours under Steve's tutelage.

Steve wore headphones, listening to the tap—called a touch by these people—in Prion's office. They had placed several devices throughout his quarters and in the rest of the compound outside Nida. The system was capable of taping three conversations at once. It was an awesome setup, arranged and controlled by the blonde woman. How in hell had that crooked-nosed Russian ever attracted her? The bastard better not look at Jade.

The live conversation Steve was hearing interested him because he raised his hand. The room became quiet.

"The banker speaketh," said Steve, flicking a switch.

Speaketh? Rimas wondered again about Steve's Texas dialect.

"I don't understand!" came a whiny voice over the main speaker. "You can't pull my funding just like that. I'm good for it. You know I'm good for it. I'm just waiting for the court to close probate. I'm the only heir."

"That's Prion," said Steve. "He's talking to the banker."

"The Michigan court has delayed the case," said the banker, also in English. "Someone intervened and produced a will. If the will is found to be genuine you will not inherit your son's estate. You are not in the will."

The voice recited these points as if he were repeating a well-rehearsed list. A list he expected Prion to know by now.

Prion expanded Rimas's education in American idiomatic expressions further with a long series of oaths—at volume.

"We're only halfway to the recruitment goal. How the fuck am I gonna pay these guys? I got six more waiting for flights out of New York, but I'll lose them if I don't pay their goddamned airfares. You said yourself it has to be a big enough force to make it credible."

"Numbers can be adjusted by propaganda. You have enough for the plan already. A few bodies, a few pictures are all we need."

"But will the Russians respond like you said? That Lithuanian bitch I was married to loved her village, Juodkrantė. Will they level it like you promised if it's only a small attack?"

"All we require is the provocation. But your son's will...."

They were interrupted by somebody bringing coffee and spoke little while they drank. The listeners in the safehouse likewise filled their cups.

Charlie took advantage of the pause to give a pointed look toward Jade, eyebrows raised in a question.

Skosh answered for her. "The banker flew in from Germany an hour ago. Our in-country resident loaned me some watchers, now that Kestutis is considered to have turned."

"He is a loan officer at Felixsee Bank southeast of Berlin," said Jade, reading from the screen of her notebook computer. "There is not much information about him at all, only as much as you might get from a telephone book, just phone number and street. His name is Karl Weltung."

"No, it is not," said Sergei. "I know that voice. Very scratchy and he mispronounces the 'th' sound. He is SVR. We took the same initial language course in the KGB."

Sergei paused for universal appreciation of his mastery of the 'th' sound, then continued.

"His name is Ignat Gurin. He was posted to Berlin after training."

Ahah! thought Rimas. He was right about Sergei's background, and unfortunately correct also that Kestutis was being deceived by Prion.

"Silence!" hissed Mack, pointing to the turning tape machine.

Why did they call him Misha? He was certainly not Russian.

Weltung-Gurin spoke with exaggerated patience. "From Moscow. It should have told you about the will."

"Yes, yes," said Prion. "I got the message. My damaged son left the whole jackpot to the pervert who damaged him, and killed him for all I know, though he's still alive in his filth while my son is dead. I sent Kestutis to take care of it. He couldn't find him or the will and came back with some weird story about a guy named Mack…"

"Mack?" interrupted the banker. "Was he Austrian?"

"I don't know what he was, but Kestutis is convinced he's some kind of fighter. An older guy like him, though, so he can't be that good."

"If it is who I think it is, he is better than good. Did Kestutis mention any Americans?"

"Just an American government guy he was appointed to work with on a secret project. He said the guy looks like he's Asian. What? Why do you look like that? What's wrong?"

After a pause, Gurin said in a low voice, almost a mutter, "Charlemagne's babysitter."

As the listeners and their equipment fell silent during a long pause, Rimas enjoyed watching Sergei squirm a bit under the questioning stares of both Mack and Charlie. The Russian shrugged, then nodded.

"Skosh has been our babysitter only four years," he said. "If Gurin knows who he is, it means that he is still active. This must be an SVR operation."

TWENTY-NINE

All eyes turned to Charlemagne's babysitter, even before Steve returned to the headphones and turned off the speaker at Mack's signal. At first, Skosh thought they might be blaming his noticeable presence for a material disadvantage he couldn't see. So what if some fucking SVR toad knew who he was? At least they were the acknowledged enemy, not so-called allies who might kill him at any moment. Besides, Mack and Charlie had worse security concerns to worry about now, like how they were going to face some forty fighters within what Skosh estimated to be the next twenty hours.

He had begun a review of possible scenarios when he noticed the continued silence and felt the blue eyes burning through his consciousness like lasers. He returned the gaze with a slight questioning head tilt but found the answer as if by telepathy.

"You don't need my password," he told Mack.

"Do you prefer I get it from Jade? Which of you would better weather the storm caused by a breach, should it be discovered?"

"You're forcing me into a moral dilemma. That's unfair since you engineered it."

"Fair? Do you think facing forty men when we are six, with one of us untried, is fair odds? Yet, we agreed only because the provision in the agreement that you say I 'engineered' makes it barely possible. When I looked into your government's proposal, I requested that provision and was as surprised as you were when it was agreed to. The money is nothing compared with the information. We had no choice but to take the commission. Then you, Skosh, 'engineered' a way to deny me the access we need to succeed, to stay alive."

Skosh closed his eyes, sighed, and nodded slightly.

"Jade can …"

Jade was staring at him wide-eyed.

"Jade cannot," said Mack immediately. "Her assistant does not have access. It may not be in her system, and its classification will be too high for her little encryption device. Did you think I do not understand how you are organized? How your office operates?"

Skosh had often seen him hot with anger. He had felt the power in his fists when Mack thought it was the only way to gain his attention. He had been lectured and insulted too many times to count, but he realized he was not the only person in the room holding his breath. The entire team, even Charlie, had become cautious before the smoking volcano that was Mack.

"What, exactly, do you need?" He managed to keep from squeaking it, but only barely.

"I need the message to Gurin from Moscow, the one he forwarded to Prion, both the original in Russian and the English translation Prion received."

Skosh had seen others in this position. He knew Mack had compromised his predecessor in some way. Was this how he'd done it? He had also saved the man's life and the lives of his family. Skosh loved this job, with all its difficulty, and had nothing else apart from martial arts to go to. Maybe he could open a dojo, teach kids….

Fuck.

But then he would be free of Candace, free to date Jade if she were willing. He looked at her. She was as breathless as the others. She better not faint. Would she date a washed-up babysitter? What if they prosecuted him? They wouldn't. They would not want the agreement brought into evidence.

They might have a different solution.

Fuck.

There was no vertical way out, only horizontal, with or without his blood supply. He understood bleeding out could be relatively painless. Bullets were faster, though.

"I will spare Candace Seston," said Mack, still quiet, still seething, "though I owe you nothing in return for abiding by the agreement she arranged to punish you. She is a worthless exchange for what you imagine to be your honor, Skosh, and will not survive you otherwise. I am not fond of anyone who costs me a good babysitter."

Skosh dug deep. He had reconciled himself to his ending and felt free to go at any time. But as selfish and venal as Candace was, her stupidity did not warrant a death sentence.

Mack snorted. He was becoming impatient and, with a show of reluctance, put one more thing on the table.

"I will not ask more from you in future."

"You won't ask because I don't have a future."

"You need not die painlessly or quickly, you know. We will do what we can. That is all I can give you." He turned to Mara. "Allow Jade to use your machine."

Fucking mind reader.

Jade turned to stare at him, eyes bulging, asking for permission to do what Mack had ordered and no doubt trying to tell him to say yes. Hadn't she already made a deal with Mack? But it didn't include her password. If he couldn't let Candace die of stupidity, he couldn't let Jade suffer unemployment because of his failure. He nodded to her, and she took the seat Mara was offering.

He stood next to her as she brought up the sign-in screen and looked up at him, then vacated the seat when he touched her shoulder. He sat; he typed his log-in and password, and he left the seat to Mara.

Seven minutes later, the printer came to life.

THIRTY

She wanted only to curl up all alone under that duvet with a working lock on the door. Exhaustion born of extreme tension made Jade's legs weak, and the words alone and working were mere myths in this new universe of deception and necessity. Maybe she could downgrade the adjective meant for the lock to functional, but with this crew, that would be equally inaccurate. She doubted a bank vault could keep them out. She had just watched them penetrate her vault, almost silently and with superb efficiency, in seven minutes.

Mack disappeared upstairs and came into the main room carrying a heavy overcoat. He put it on as he crossed the room toward her but spared one cold glance at Skosh, making Jade wonder if this was it, though she still could not believe completely in the reality of lethal danger. He had done what Mack wanted, hadn't he? It was all too much like a movie, except everything was grubbier and more complicated and less explained.

Instead of sitting in a comfortable chair eating popcorn, she stood in the midst of chaos, purposeful but incomprehensible, because it was conducted in multiple languages, none of which she spoke. She regretted the emptiness in her coffee mug and the beginning fullness in her bladder but forgot about both when she saw Skosh blanch under Mack's glance. It confirmed to her imagination that this might be the big 'it' for her boss, even though he had caved.

But Mack passed him by, still buttoning his coat. He grasped her upper arm. Skosh sent out a stream of vehement German as Mack swept the rug aside and pushed her through. She caught a glimpse and heard a scuffle when Steve intercepted Skosh.

"Put on your coat." Mack took her jacket off the door and threw it at her.

Jade still held her mug, and anyway, her hands shook too much for the buttons. Mack took the cup from her, placed it on the table, picked up and opened the coat while she put each arm into a sleeve.

"Do you have a scarf? Gloves?"

She nodded and looked at the cardboard box in the corner that provided a form of organization in the tiny room. He pointed toward it with an open palm indicating she should put them on, but she remained paralyzed. Mack rolled his eyes upward and sighed. He grabbed her pink mittens and Skosh's black scarf out of the box and put them in her hands. Then he buttoned her coat.

She considered, surely, it would not be important to dress warmly for the big 'it,' would it? And what kind of assassin buttons the coat of the quivering victim before doing the deed? The absurdity of her situation clashed with the very real danger all around her and gave her the strength to don her pink mittens on her own.

As Mack pulled her outside, cold air struck her face while disordered reality crowded her mind. This was no neat movie plot with a foreordained ending. Back in that pair of safehouses, any of them, all of them, each of them could die very soon, she realized. Odds favored that at least one of them would.

She watched the toes of her boots as they shuffled over familiar paving stones near the dry dock. Mack halted at Skosh's favorite stopping point but remained silent. Forcing herself to look up, she stared into those blue eyes.

"Skosh is no longer in danger from me," said Mack. "It is time to discuss how you will fulfill your part of our bargain."

The nerve of the man! Anger became a great aid in overcoming fear. It gave Jade's reply all the bite she could wish for in her words.

"He's out of danger because you won. You trapped and defeated him. I had nothing to do with it, nor did our so-called agreement, which ends right here and now."

She stamped her foot.

The bastard laughed out loud, took her arm, and began moving further down the walkway before he spoke again, still chuckling here and there.

"The gossip you shared with me helped me convince him to behave rationally. I commend you, but now that I have arranged for him, and possibly the rest of us, to continue living, I am calling in your debt to me. You said, as I recall, 'anything' and also 'name it.' I am naming it."

Anger gave way again to fear, but maybe it was adrenaline that was speeding up her thinking.

"Surely, you wouldn't want to cheat on Alex."

"Cheat on? I am unfamiliar with the expression. You are not suggesting I should forego a pleasure merely because Alex is not here to provide it, are you?"

He gave her that wicked, boyish smile again. She decided it would be tactless to mention his age explicitly, so she reworded her next argument.

"I'm younger than Charlie."

Realizing too late that this was worse, she tried and failed to stammer a retraction.

He laughed again, then became suddenly serious.

"You always divert me, Jade, but I am not here to be entertained. I will hold you to the agreement, but not for myself."

This made her blanch, unless he meant Skosh, which seemed unlikely. She held her breath.

"Breathe, Jade. I have no desire to see you faint. Now listen to me."

She looked up and saw no hint of a smile; the eyes had hardened as well. She made a show of taking a deep breath.

"Good. I transfer your generous offer to Rimas. In a little while he will need incentive, and then if he lives, in a few hours he will require your understanding. You will give him both. Whatever he wishes, you will say yes. He is young and fit and reasonably good-looking. It should not be difficult for you."

How very like a man, thought Jade. Sex need not mean anything beyond the appearance of the parties. She was arrested by the words, 'if he lives' and began to worry about Rimas. She liked him enough to be concerned but not enough to bargain with a devil as she had for Skosh. At first, she swallowed this instruction as being not so bad if it got her off the hook but then found herself wondering about her own sexual attitudes. Rimas was rather delightful.

Mack had watched her face, no doubt reading each thought as it traveled across her brain, and as if satisfied with her conclusion, began a lecture about how to behave in the next few hours. Most of it swept by her, but three things stuck in her mind along with his low purring voice as he said them.

"Do not become emotional."

"Follow Charlie's orders exactly."

And finally, "Keep your hands where they can be seen at all times, unless they are tied behind you, of course."

"Then this is end game?" she asked.

She had surprised him into another wicked smile.

"You must know you will not succeed with Skosh," he said.

She tried not to show her disappointment but knew she failed. "He is married then?"

"No. Worse. He is honorable. But to answer your first question, we have entered the middle game. There are still too many pieces on the board."

As Jade tilted her head, puzzled, he answered the unspoken question.

"Our opening succeeded. I shall call it Mack's Gambit. We are now in a position to win the advantage through a series of exchanges. The next move will involve our knight, Rimas. Give him an enthusiastic yes."

She felt bruised, unwashed, exhausted, and ugly. Enthusiasm seemed a pipe dream. Mack stopped and turned her to face him. He was not smiling.

"The end game, when it comes, may require a sacrifice of one or more of our pieces."

THIRTY-ONE

"If you are Austrian, why do you speak American English?" Rimas asked Charlie.

They walked slowly down a path in a small park by the shore. Rimas noticed Mack leading Jade toward the dry dock.

"My stepmother is American," said Charlie. "But what you want to know is why Sergei is on the team. He is married to my sister. The family is like a mini-United Nations, though without the peace-keeping. Any more questions?"

"You are a wizard."

"No, I just watch people carefully. You will pick it up soon enough. If you live."

Rimas raised his brows in alarm and Charlie continued. "It is a superstition of ours to never assume we will live through the next op. Kestutis gave you the physical skills you will need, and maybe mental strength, but we also have our own ways that you must learn if you are to join us and also...."

"And also if I live," interrupted Rimas.

Charlie smiled. Then he told Rimas what it was he might not live through.

"Be sure to go to the Lithuanians first, then the Americans. Who knows, you might be able to walk out again. If that's the case, disappear quickly, before they can think. I know Kestutis taught you how to move through the forest. We will do what we can for you if you're taken, but it will take time."

Rimas nodded. "I am prepared. If Kestutis...."

"Don't count on Kestutis. He may not be there. We think he is still in Šiauliai."

"He will be there—eventually. I know him. He will not stay away. The others will...."

"Stop dreaming, Rimas. It is not a good habit. Look, there's Jade." Charlie pointed to her as she walked with Mack. "Rest your mind with her. She is very real and if you just think about her, it won't deflect your path; it won't make you add or subtract from the plan. You have memorized it?"

Rimas nodded as he watched Jade walk back to the house. He doubted she was safe with this team, but the thing called safety was relative after all, and Charlie was right. He had no control over what Kestutis might do. He also had no intention of passing up Charlie's implied promise of better luck with Jade.

…

"Lunch is due in five fucking minutes," Skosh hissed at Jade as she came in the door. He glowered at Mack behind her. He knew how to lose a sparring match with grace but surrendering his password had not gone smoothly down his ethical gullet. He would need copious antacids to keep the resentment down.

He added an insolent glare to his glower.

Mack answered with a silent, cold challenge.

Skosh did not feel that crazy. He looked away.

That the son of a bitch had something up his sleeve regarding Jade had not escaped him. Preserving his skin was suddenly not enough. He needed to preserve hers as well, or he knew, as surely as he knew his name, that he could never live with what he had done to her.

Mack's low voice reached his ears despite the chaos in the room.

"She is in no more danger than you are, Skosh."

"If that's the case, then use me instead."

"There are some things only she can do." Mack's chuckle as he said this told Skosh everything he never wanted to know.

"So Rimas is joining Charlemagne," he said through clenched teeth. "Or are you just using him?"

"Yes, if he lives, he will join us."

"So both."

"He is a fighter, Skosh, trained by Kestutis, one of the best in this part of the world. His eyes are open. You need not fear for him. He will find plenty of that on his own."

"Mack, you know it's part of my job to minimize the impact on the surrounding population. That young man is a Lithuanian citizen. If you're sending him on some suicide mission, I need to make him aware of it."

"Charlie has fully briefed him. Rimas will play an important role. As I told Jade, Rimas is our knight. There are some moves only he can make."

Why, thought Skosh, has Jade been made privy to information he had to pry from Mack? Because she plays chess? And how did they find another language, though expressed with English words, that allows them to communicate with so much nuance?

He resolved to take up the game.

If he lived.

. . .

"What? Are you my pimp now?"

Jade risked the acid in her voice because she knew she had the higher moral ground. Minimally higher, like maybe a millimeter.

Charlie pulled the last hairpin from her coiled braid and laid the pins on the dresser.

"I want him to think about only you and his task. You are competing with Kestutis for space in his mind. Your hair is an advantage. Use it."

He picked up her brush and began arranging her hair about her shoulders.

"I tried putting makeup on the bruises," said Jade. "It made them worse."

"He won't be thinking about your bruises."

She felt his icy cold stare as he held her shoulders, boring his words into her with such solemnity it made her shudder.

"This op is his first and it is difficult. He needs a reason to survive. You will have five minutes to provide it."

As he turned to leave the bedroom, she couldn't help herself. The way they all took her obedience for granted grated on her.

"That's it? That's all I get from you? Not even a 'thank you for your service?'"

He turned at the door, eyebrows raised. "I will be happy to give you much more than that."

"A sim ... simple thank you will suffice."

The bastard smiled and left the room without saying anything.

...

Skosh saw the minimal lift of Charlie's chin as he came through the rug into the team's larger room. Rimas stood by the computer, dressed now in winter forest camouflage and armed with a semi-auto pistol and an earbud. Sergei was dressed like his twin. The two were about to leave, but Rimas went through the rug alone.

Skosh followed him, stood in the kitchen, and waited. It took no more than two minutes for the bedroom door to open. Rimas had the same grim set to his face as he left that Skosh had worn when he prepared himself for death only a few hours ago. He sincerely hoped the young man would live and fleetingly wondered what kind of specialist he would become. Wired and crazy? Silent and sinister? Analytical and cold? Or some new combination not yet present on the team?

He stepped into the bedroom.

For a moment, he could only gaze at her. Who ties her flannel shirt tails at the waist during an op? Jade does. He had never known a woman so completely out of her depth yet who could remain herself, from kitten heels to a flannel fashion statement.

Why was her hair down? Stupid question. Another confirmation of his suspicions. She had just been kissed, judging by the redness around her lips and the way she licked them. Kissed hard.

She smiled at him.

"Jade," he said after a deep breath, "I know what they're up to. I suspect it's their idea of psychological support, specialist style. You've been pressured, threatened, and tricked. I want you to know you do not have to do this. I will take you out of here right now, bring you to Vilnius, and put you on a flight home."

The smile disappeared.

"At what cost, Skosh? Mack told Kestutis you would die for me. I won't let you do that. As costs are counted, mine is very light. It is not optimal, but certainly not unpleasant. Relax. We will get through this."

He kissed her then. Properly. Stealing an illicit moment from Rimas, from the team, from grim reality.

THIRTY-TWO

Rimas had more trouble with the Americans than he expected. To be sure, the Lithuanian fighters read with a critical air the printout of the message from Moscow that he brought, but it held too many genuine marks and Russian abbreviations to be dismissed outright as a forgery.

Kestutis was not there, but thanks to Feliksas, the group recognized Rimas as his protégé, giving his words added credibility.

"Who are you working for then?" asked a suspicious younger man. "The Americans?"

"They are not Americans, but they are here with an American government agent."

"Are they Russian?"

"No."

Rimas considered it wiser to leave off explaining Sergei.

"Have you seen Kestutis?" asked another man.

"Not since yesterday."

Again, details seemed inadvisable. There had been no curiosity about his bruised face.

"What does this mean about Prion's funding?" asked a more seasoned fighter. "We carry our own equipment. He does not supply it."

"The Americans are paid," explained Rimas.

"Those thieves in that other building? They are being paid while we are not?"

"No," said a tall man at the back. "That is the point of the message, Jonas. They are not being paid. It means they are not likely to stay. We will be left on our own, to be slaughtered. Or, I should say, you will be on your own because I am leaving."

Eleven more Lithuanians joined him, shouldering knapsacks and AK-47s as they made their way into the night. Rimas told them about a convenient hole in the fence behind their barrack and they melted into the forest. Two more followed them, deputed by the others to find Kestutis in Šiauliai and show him the message from Moscow. Three remained to wait for him before making a decision.

Rimas was not entirely sure of one of them and was careful to check his back while making his silent way to the American barrack.

There, he had more difficulty being believed, but there was a phone in this building. When one of the men reached his bank just before close of business in a place called Birmingham, he hung up the phone, turned to the others, and announced, "I didn't get the dough."

Rimas worked out how many English words for money he now knew while another three men called their banks to confirm the first man's result. They began packing. The exodus was both less orderly and less complete, with only ten gone and eight waiting for the phone when a large man came through the door.

"What the fuck?"

"We ain't been paid, Lowell."

"So what? It's only temporary. Who the fuck is this?"

All eyes turned to Rimas. He would have drawn the gun Charlie had given him, but Lowell had already swung the muzzle of his rifle in his direction. Rimas was getting sick of surrender but swallowed his self-disgust as the first blows reminded him that he was still alive.

THIRTY-THREE

Dinner arrived in four rectangular tubs covered with foil. Jade thought it odd that just when they had plenty of table space, the food took up almost none at all. All the gear, the computer, radio equipment, and most of the sensor apparatus had been transferred that afternoon to an old rust bucket of a van that she heard Skosh assure Charlie would run like a top. Charlie gave his trademark belligerent stare in reply and Skosh laughed. His mood had lightened.

Jade gathered four of her large wooden spoons and placed one in each bin. These contained nothing but the delicious meat pies in pastry called *kibinai*, a specialty of Lithuanian Tatars, Muslims who had come to the country as early as the fourteenth century. The caterers provided one tub each of chicken, beef, pork, and lamb. Jade's spoons were surplus to the team's needs. They grabbed the pies by hand and ate them standing at the table before grabbing more. Well, Mara used a spoon to fish out a whole meat pie from the remnants caused by all the hand-grabbing but then ate it the same way as her teammates.

They seemed different somehow, Steve and Charlie especially, but also Mara. Her blonde hair had been pulled back tightly, accentuating the fine bones of her face and exceptional brightness in her green eyes. It was the brightness that caught Jade's attention. They all had it, even Mack, though he had not dressed like the others, in forest camouflage.

The portable radio Mack held squawked. He caught Charlie's eye, who then pointed at Skosh and Jade.

"You two. I'll see you in the bedroom, now."

"Which bedroom would that be?" asked Skosh, with the merest hint of insolence.

"Jade's bedroom, the one that does not smell like a pig sty. Now."

They stood by the dresser as Charlie closed the door.

"Rimas is taken. You two will bargain for him."

Jade gasped. Skosh raised a fist.

"You mother fucking son of a bitch! You assured me Jade would not be used as a dangle."

"You are confusing me with my father. I gave no assurances whatsoever."

Motionless and menacing, Charlie's voice held all the venom required by the occasion. He continued softly, making Jade suppress shudders after every other word.

"Here's what you're going to do. Start by cleaning yourselves up. Skosh, go shave and put on your best suit. Jade, wear makeup. I don't care that it won't cover the bruises, make it look like you tried. Put your hair up and put on something stylish. Those little boots with the funny heels will do nicely. Did you bring a skirt by any chance?"

And so on. Jade dressed, hearing brief snatches of the conversation in the bathroom next door as Charlie explained the plan to Skosh while he shaved. Skosh interrupted him frequently and with vehemence, but Charlie replied with quiet force. She could not understand the words.

"I would never …" insisted Skosh.

"You will this time," said Charlie.

In the car, Jade smoothed a wrinkle in the vintage designer stirrup slacks she found at a flea market and had worn on the airplane. They tucked neatly into her favorite half-boots. The makeup made her feel like a painted clown because it was excessive, but Charlie insisted.

"You know," said Skosh, turning onto the road into Nida, "I don't know what the real plan is. No doubt there will be double-dealing and this is only a conjecture. Treachery is likely to be what the targets want, but Mack is probably in on it, so Charlie's right. Save your emotion for Rimas and play it up when the time comes."

"Why do you think Mack is in on it?"

"Because I'm pretty sure Charlie would never betray his dad and that's what it feels like. Mack told you not to be emotional. He didn't mean don't feel something for Rimas. They want you to do that. So he probably meant don't let your emotions about him cloud your obedience to Charlie."

Jade thought it more likely that Mack had been referring to how she felt about Skosh.

"If I know you're sweet on the old guy," he continued, "he knows it, too."

It was time to change the subject.

"Charlie noticed my designer boots."

"Charlie notices everything. Don't be so pleased with yourself."

"I'm not. I'm pleased with the price I paid for them. They were next to nothing when you count the T-shirts they came with. Those were useless, so I cut them up for rags."

She prattled to pass the time, to squeeze the situation into a dark corner of her mind. He listened the way all men listen to such things: not at all.

Skosh showed his passport to a camera at the gate of Prion's compound. It swung open.

Thugs was the word Jade would have used to describe their escorts into what appeared to be the main building. It was the largest wooden structure surrounded by a number of smaller sheds, all of them dotted among tall pines with straight, bare trunks. The hoodlums frisked them both for weapons. Skosh lost his H&K semi-auto pistol, and Jade thought the man with his hands on her lingered too long in some places. He was ugly as sin with a bald head and ink all over his face, but it was the leer that made him especially loathsome.

There weren't too many people around as they crossed a small, paved area in front of the building. Inside, a long, narrow hallway ran through the center, with four doors opening onto it, staggered, two on each side, and a grander (had it been painted) wooden double door at the end. It opened and they were ushered into the presence of Earl Prion, father of the late rock star, Tommy Taurus.

The desk was too grandiose for him. It made him look like a janitor, here to clean the furniture on behalf of an executive. The tall, well-built man standing to one side fit that role better. He wore a well-cut suit and wire-rimmed glasses and held a briefcase in one hand.

"What do you want?" Prion's voice sounded peevish.

"First, I'd like my sidearm back," said Skosh with some heat. "It cost a packet and I've been authorized to carry it by the Lithuanian Defense Ministry. I'm here on official United States government business and don't expect to be treated like a criminal by a fellow American."

Prion pursed his lips and looked to the guy in the suit for guidance.

"Tell us why you are here," said the man smoothly. He had an accent that faintly reminded Jade of Sergei.

"Who are you?" Skosh remained belligerent.

"My name is Karl Weltung. And you are?"

"John Nakamura."

Jade wondered if Skosh saw Weltung's reaction the way she did. She understood he was a major player in this secret game, but he betrayed himself like an amateur. She would have done a better job not reacting to Skosh's name. He opened his eyes wide and blinked slowly to give himself time to think before he spoke.

"What do you want?"

Skosh played the bluff, harried government bureaucrat to a tee, explaining how he was responsible for this chit of a secretary who'd fallen in love with some Lithuanian who was here in the compound, and could she see him?

Thus began negotiations.

THIRTY-FOUR

They produced a beaten and trussed Rimas. Skosh could see a few more bruises on his face, and he limped a bit, but he was alive. Jade made a show of sobbing loudly and trying to run to him. He joined the drama and held her back. He was not about to let her go anywhere near the brutes standing to either side of Rimas.

"She is the only person who thinks he's important," insisted Skosh. "Just let him go so she can patch him up. He has no power to threaten you."

"Then how did he know I lost my funding?" screamed Prion.

Gurin raised a hand in warning, and Prion corrected himself, speaking quickly and shuffling a pile of papers on the desk to mask his nervousness.

"I mean that's what he told my men, showing them a forged message about a purely routine holdup in the final funds. Right guys?" He looked to the two men holding Rimas, who nodded.

"Overzealous in your interests maybe," said Skosh, "mistakenly trying to help you, but essentially harmless. Let him go home to lick his wounds. We are in-country on other business and pose no threat to you."

Gurin's shoulders twitched. So did one eyebrow. His dark eyes caught the American in a steady glare as he spoke quickly.

"I believe the popular English expression is 'bullshit,' Nakamura. I know who you are, what you are. This man may be unimportant, as you say, but if he is connected to you, I must know how. He will tell us—eventually."

"He knows nothing. He's just an interpreter for Miss Wilburton, who is my administrative assistant."

Skosh had also dropped the pretended bluffness. He tensed his muscles while loosening the fingers at his sides. He was ready to fight.

Prion stood with the tip of his tongue showing through his teeth, moving only his eyes from Gurin to Skosh as they negotiated.

"I presume he has eyes and ears," said Gurin. "He will remember what he has seen and heard. We will help his memory."

"But he has no real information. Let him go and keep me instead."

Gurin's eyes opened wide again. He took his time with his next careful suggestion.

"I know you can offer a bigger prize. Kestutis has described him to Mr. Prion."

Prion tilted his head and wrinkled his brow, trying to remember everything Kestutis had told them.

"What prize, Weltung? What the hell are you talking about?"

The banker held up one hand to silence him.

"Let me handle this, Earl."

"I want to know what you're talking about. This is my operation, damn it."

"It's mine now. This is beyond you. It will be the highlight of my career, even if the other fails."

Gurin instructed the guards to leave the room with their prisoner, bypassing Prion entirely in his haste to secure the bigger prize.

Prion nodded at the guards, pretending he still held authority as they turned away. When they had gone, he gave his banker an ingratiating smile.

"Very wise, Karl," he said. "It's better that they not know anything Kestutis said. I don't entirely trust him."

Jade had stopped crying, leaving her mouth open in surprise at Gurin's suggestion.

"You see," Gurin told Skosh with a satisfied smile, "even your assistant understands. She was there when he and Kestutis met. Perhaps I should keep her."

Skosh frowned in dismay. Charlie had foreseen every move.

"What do you propose?"

THIRTY-FIVE

R imas thought he must be dreaming as they shoved him toward the van.

"Oh my darling, what have they done to you?" said Jade, running alongside him.

Darling?

The van's back door swung open with four men already inside. Jade kept talking.

"You look terrible, but I will nurse you. I'm taking you out of here."

Terrible? He had an extra bruise or two from the futile fight he put up when the Americans seized him—for the sake of self-respect—but nothing more since she saw him in Prion's office. The real interrogation had not yet begun. He gave her his best question-mark look, hoping she could read it. He had been held in another room during what seemed an eon squeezed into half an hour, while Skosh and Gurin bargained.

"I've arranged your release," Jade said. "We just have to make some arrangements at my house. These men are going to assist us, and once that's done, they'll let you go. There. At the house."

He read her look as meaning 'play along; this is mandatory.' He played along.

They were both bundled into the back of the van with the four heavily muscled men. His hands remained tied behind him, but hers were free. She kept them in front of her, visible. Two more men sat up front. Rimas ventured a question, focusing on Jade because if he looked at the leering gargoyle next to her, he knew he would explode.

"Will Mr. Nakamura meet us at your house?"

"No, my dear, he elected to remain with Mr. Prion to finalize the arrangements for your release."

Six men. Skosh held hostage. It was all wrong, but Jade's plastic smile demanded cooperation. He returned an equally fake grimace.

The van parked under the trees, twenty meters behind the house. Their six-man escort stood hesitating, arguing and asking the same questions repeatedly. Six men, one woman, and Rimas with his hands tied behind him stood freezing in clouds of breathy argument.

"Look," Jade said with some heat. "I told you Mr. Nakamura dismantled the sensors. See? I have the part that controls the alarm system."

She pulled a metal computer part from the back pocket of her slim corduroy pants. A ribbon connector dangled from it. Rimas recognized the used part she had bought during their early shopping trip in Klaipeda. Why, he wondered, were six fighters worried about the sensors? Who were they after? He became uneasy and uncertain. So far, he found nobody around him to be trustworthy—not the Americans, not Kestutis, not the girl he had kissed and wanted to kiss again. He could handle violence; conjecture would kill him.

After ten minutes of noisy education in American words, they left Rimas standing in the snow, still tied, with one man as a guard. The other five accompanied Jade through the back door of the team's safehouse.

His concern for her lasted no more than a moment after the door closed. He heard a soft pop-zip and watched his guard fall with a thud, a neat hole in his temple. Sergei stepped out of the brush holding a knife. He cut Rimas's bonds and shoved a suppressed MP5 submachine gun into his hands.

"I thought they would never make a decision," he said in Russian. "Come. Help me hide him."

"Jade …"

"Jade will be okay. She will see a good fight. We cannot stay for it."

THIRTY-SIX

Jade had a front-row seat, or rather, stand. They left Rimas outside, guarded by one man, then pushed her ahead of them, storming single file through the team's narrow kitchen, past the massive brick stove, and into the main room.

Mack jumped from his chair and whirled to face them, gun in hand. He shot the man behind her as Jade stepped to her left in order not to be in the way. The next man also moved left and stayed behind her.

The third man ran at Mack, leaping as high as the ceiling allowed and swinging one leg in a wide arc. Mack blocked the kick before it could reach his head, held the foot, and shoved the man into the table that once held Mara's computer. He slid along the top, scattering empty tubs of kibinai remnants, but was on his feet again beginning another leap when Mack shoved his knuckles into the man's throat, throwing him back a second time. This time he fell, stunned and struggling for breath until Mack's bullet found him and ended the struggle.

Numbers four and five wasted no time. They dashed around the bodies and came at him from both sides. By now, Mack had his back to a wall as the man on his right grabbed his arm, beating it against the wall until the SIG Sauer fell to the floor. The one on the left kicked the gun out of reach. Mack pulled out a knife with his left hand, swung into the man holding his right arm, and kneed him in the groin. As the man doubled over, Mack pointed his knife upward and shoved it into his chest. He fell face up, the knife implanted to its hilt.

"Fuck," said the man to the left, pulling his gun out of a hip holster.

"Don't!" shouted the thug behind Jade. He grabbed her arm. "Weltung wants him alive. We can't shoot him, but he didn't say nothin' about her."

He pressed the muzzle of his weapon against Jade's temple.

She refused to die with her eyes closed and so had them open to watch Mack surrender to two American hoodlums. She gasped, suddenly understanding what Skosh had been trying to tell her in the car. He must have known about this and thought Mack also knew about the attack, but now he had lost the fight, and it was because of her. She reviewed all the instructions. Each word Charlie said came back to her with perfect clarity. She followed all of them. She had not moved. Her hands were visible. She had controlled her emotions, and still, Mack lost.

He said he would not die for her, but she was alive, and he was captured.

And now, so was she. The two goons had plans of their own. After a disgusting conversation, they decided to tell Prion it was a trap and explain they kept both her and Rimas for that reason. Then, they would await their opportunity.

They took some revenge on Mack, inflicting severe bruising as payback for their dead comrades. While they occupied themselves with this, she slipped through the rug, out the front door, and ran as fast as her boots would let her along the side of the house, behind the wood pile, and into the forest, where she tripped over a body and fell flat on her face in the snow.

The sound of voices kept her down and still, raising her head just enough to watch the clearing beyond the trees that sheltered her and the grisly thing that had brought her down. She saw them frog march Mack, his hands tightly zip-tied behind him, out the back door.

"Where the fuck is Gansen?"

They called the name, followed a few footsteps they could see in the deeper parts of the snow leading into the dark brush under the trees, but did not dare go further lest they lose the prize they had come for. With a shrug, the two men decided Gansen had legged it.

If this was Gansen, wondered Jade, where was Rimas? She was terrified they would kill Mack in front of her because she had done something wrong, though she didn't know what, not that she ever knew anything, but she knew now she didn't want him to die. Not him, not Rimas, not any of them. And above all, not Skosh. She wanted to apologize as a way to erase the past and make everything better, but Mack was captured, Skosh held hostage, and the team nowhere to be seen.

…

"Location?" Michael used English for Rimas's sake. By now, Sergei should have given him another earbud. Also by now the two should have been at the team's van. A surge of foreboding intruded on his thoughts. He quashed it.

Sergei answered the call.

"There was a shot, but now nothing. They have not come out. What should we do?"

It had been Michael's idea to use his father as bait. His idea and his plan, a plan without much flexibility in the timing. Michael closed his eyes. Silence took hold of everyone in the van. Mara avoided eye contact. Misha was her father, too, but the operation must come first.

"Get back here," he said.

"On our way."

Michael wanted to scream loud, elemental, belligerent fury at the malevolence of a destiny that would make his father the earliest victim of his solo leadership.

Sergei's panting voice again came to his ear. "Another shot …"

"Get here."

The order came automatically, without hesitation. A supreme test of ruthless leadership, and he had passed it. Michael marked the moment for thought later, not letting it delay the calculations he needed to make now.

"Drive," he told Steve in the seat next to him as Sergei and Rimas fell inside and slammed shut the back door. Mara came forward and lifted one earphone.

"The watcher at the ferry says Kestutis has boarded the boat."

Michael turned in this seat, calculations finished, necessary re-arrangements decided.

He looked at Rimas. "You will wait for Kestutis beside the road. You know his car?"

Rimas nodded.

"Stay with him. Do what you can."

The young man nodded again.

"Pull over three kilometers before the compound to let Rimas out," Michael told Steve. "Then bring us to the departure point. You'll run to the front gate and watch for the van Sergei said the tangos are driving."

"Me?"

"Yes, you. I want to know if and when it gets there. If it's not there after half an hour, take your position by the American barrack."

Michael turned to Mara, who stood holding the back of his seat.

"You and I will go to the Lithuanian barrack. Three of them are still there."

Steve interrupted. "I thought I …"

"Change of plan," Michael said with gritted teeth. He made a mental note to address this creeping democratic tendency in the team. "Mara is more likely to persuade them to leave before the shooting starts."

Not that Steve deserved an explanation.

"I don't know any Lithuanian," said Mara.

"Use Russian. They all speak at least some."

Michael looked Steve in the eye as he spoke his next order.

"I need you to clear the American barrack. When we're done with the Lithuanians, I'll send Mara to back you up before I quietly take out as many as I can in the main building prior to the start of gunfire. It's a long hallway with too many doors and may take time. You will begin the op. Wait for her to get in position."

Steve's answering smile confirmed Michael's dispositions. The man loved a firefight and Michael was happy to oblige. Unless the rank-and-file tangos were at least half as good as Steve, which was unlikely, they had no chance. He turned to Sergei last.

"I am guessing you did not retrieve my father's weapons."

"We did not go in."

Michael nodded. "Assuming he is a prisoner and that Skosh will do as he's been told, both will need weapons. Take one of the spare semi-autos and a knife out of the weapons locker and an extra MP5. You'll meet Skosh and then back me up as I come out of that building."

"Yes." Sergei hesitated. "I am sorry …"

"For what?" Michael hoped the glare he gave would stop them all from dwelling on it. They had no time for distraction. Sergei nodded slightly, swallowed, and looked away.

THIRTY-SEVEN

Rimas stepped out from under the trees and onto the road leading to Nida just as Kestutis's car approached.

"Where are the others who went to get you?" he asked as he settled into the passenger seat of his mentor's car.

"They came to inform me, not to get me. I let them go on their way."

"Then why are you headed for Nida?"

"To confront Prion. The message you brought appears genuine, but it could be a forgery."

"If it is," said Rimas, "this is too complicated to be Russian."

"How so?" countered Kestutis.

"A Russian rescued me from Prion."

"There you are. The Russians want us to abandon Prion's attack on Kaliningrad. They are using you as a pawn."

"No, Kestutis, they want Prion to attack. They intend to use his attack as an excuse to invade us. Sergei—that is the man who rescued me—allowed me to hear a tape of Weltung explaining it to Prion. I learned their voices very well when they held me. I am not mistaken."

Kestutis scowled. "But Prion loves Lithuania. Why would he work for an invasion?"

"He hates Lithuania." Rimas followed this statement with the history of Tommy Prion and his brother Antanas.

"Why do you trust such people?" demanded Kestutis. "They are unnatural."

"Because I know my brother. He does not lie."

"But the Russian...."

"Is on the team that will kill Prion. I have been invited to join them."

Kestutis pulled off the road and into heavy brush growing under young trees.

"Team? Then he is the man I remember. They have always been anti-Soviet. But I must confront Prion to see for myself if you are correct. Why does this team want you?"

He climbed out and set off into the forest. Rimas followed like the puppy he knew he was.

"Because you trained me."

"Thank you for the flattery, but you will learn how little I have taught you in comparison with what will be expected of you. You have never killed. They are experts."

Kestutis halted, listening. Rimas heard it, too, sounds of movement through the undergrowth, then voices. As the noises grew louder, he recognized his own language. Kestutis pulled out a handgun and stepped out into the path of two men. Rimas recognized them as two of the stalwarts who had refused to believe the message he brought them.

"What the hell are you doing, blundering through the forest like a bloody herd of elephants?" said Kestutis.

"We are leaving," said one of the men. "Something is about to happen, and we have no protection. Vytautas is dead. A woman shot him. A girl. Just like that! In the chest. I'm sure he meant only to frighten her, but he got no further than taking his rifle off the locker. He was always a hothead. But this woman and the blond man with her were cold as winter. They told us to leave, and we left. The Americans in the compound are not friends."

As the two moved on and became invisible within meters into the forest, Kestutis hung his head.

"I knew Vytautas's father," he said in a low voice. "He worried about the boy. I should not have allowed him to join Prion."

He moved southward toward the compound.

"I will go with you to confront Prion," insisted Rimas. "What is your plan?"

To his dismay, Kestutis had only skill, courage, and guilt. It would be up to Charlemagne to produce enough of a plan for a successful outcome.

If they lived.

THIRTY-EIGHT

The others were already running when Steve used his luxurious extra three minutes to tighten the Velcro on his Kevlar vest and add more magazines to his belt. The van was well hidden on the side of the road past the turnoff to Nida, less than two kilometers from Prion's compound. The short run would keep him warm. But then he would freeze as he waited for that other damned van full of tangos. Maybe it would come fast. He hoped it would come fast and that it would have Misha, alive, inside.

As if the hope had made it happen, he heard a vehicle approaching. He stepped to the edge of the forest, then out onto the road when he recognized the team's rental car, not the tango van. He saw a lone driver illuminated by the late afternoon sun and pointed his MP5 at the car.

"What the fuck are you doing?" he asked as Jade rolled down the window.

"He's been captured," she said, tears streaming down her cheeks. "It's my fault. I don't know how, but it has to be my fault."

Steve hauled her out of the car and under cover of the trees. She carried a pillowcase with something in it.

"They were ahead of you?" he asked, turning his transmitter back on, then said into the mic, "We missed them." Again looking at Jade as she shivered, he asked the main question, the one everybody wanted the answer to, "He's alive?"

Back to the microphone. "She's nodding, Michael."

She tried to hand him the pillowcase. He already had enough to carry, and one hand had hold of her arm to stop her from going anywhere. What the fuck was he going to do with a pillowcase.

"They're his." She was blubbering now. "He'll want them."

They began walking toward the compound. Steve didn't know what else to do with this extra baggage of a female. It wasn't like he could just leave her in a frozen forest with no shortage of unknown tangos lurking about, and he'd be damned if he let her anywhere near the comm equipment operating in the van at a time when they most depended on it. Michael would fry him with those blue eyes of his.

He stopped, took the pillowcase from her, and looked inside. His mind spun as it sought a way to explain this over the air. There was a long pause from Michael, then instructions for a meeting with Sergei to hand it over.

"The knife's bloody," Steve said to Jade.

"I had to pull it out of the man's chest."

"The man?"

"The one he killed. One of the ones he killed. Before they took him."

He stared at her and nearly tripped over a tree root. She had stopped crying but melted makeup made streaks down her face. Almost like camo paint. She limped because the heel of one of her too-dainty boots had broken off. If he had a nest-like snarl of hair like that, he'd probably just shave it all off. She was just fluff, wasn't she? Out of her depth, not meant to be anywhere near the likes of them, even more unsuited to an op than Claire had been.

Claire had survived. Barely.

Jade had pulled Misha's knife out of a dead man.

Women. Scary creatures. That reminded him. "What do I do with the, uh, assistant?" he said into the mic.

"Hand her over to her, um, boss—with the items to be returned. Let Skosh deal with it.

Sergei and Steve both copied.

...

"It was a trap, but we got 'im," said a heavily tattooed bruiser.

Skosh hung his head, praying this was the plan, playing it for all he was worth.

Prion narrowed his eyes, twirling a pencil in his fingers. Gurin raised his eyebrows and fairly danced where he stood, chin up and triumphant. He tilted back his head, flaring his nostrils as if sniffing an imminent kill.

"How many did you lose?" asked a more morose Prion. The twirling pencil had calmed him. He scowled.

The bruiser winced. "Four. Three dead and one missing."

"How many are left, Lowell? Altogether?"

"Nine, including me. All the Lithuanians are gone. One of them is dead, too. Jones told me on my way in."

"Dead? How?"

"Shot. Accurate, too. Right through the heart. We can't find any of the others, but Jones heard that some of 'em went to Šiauliai to talk to Kestutis. Two of 'em expected him back any minute, but now they're gone, too."

Prion turned to his banker, insistent, sweat forming on his brow. "We can rebuild. We'll just need to postpone. And, of course, we need the funds."

Gurin grimaced, brought back from euphoria only long enough to register the worsening situation, then returned to his triumph.

"But you got the man?" he asked Lowell, who nodded.

"What man?" demanded Prion, dropping the pencil. "You need me Weltung, or your plan is toast, but I can't do anything without my son's estate. Help me out here."

"The plan is nothing compared to this capture." Gurin snorted and looked again at Lowell. "Where is he? I will go as soon as we are done here."

Lowell nodded. "He's alive like you ordered. He's in the locked shed, tied tight. I set a guard. The girl and her lover are gone, though. You want I should go rough the guy up a bit?"

Skosh threw him a malevolent glance. It was his cue to act.

"I demand to see the prisoner," he said to Gurin, dropping all pretense that Prion had any authority in this situation. It gratified him to see Prion's scowl.

"The man is an American ally," Skosh continued. "I voluntarily allowed you to detain me while you sought your prize, but now you have him, I must speak to him and explain his rights so I can assure my government of his continued welfare. Have your man bring him here or escort me to a suitable place for an interview."

He hoped he sounded like he knew what he was doing. Charlie said he would find the necessary weapons when he needed them. How that was supposed to happen remained a mystery. Skosh marveled that he had been reduced to relying on that cutthroat son of Satan as he followed this goon down the long hallway.

Then, as Lowell passed a door on the right, it opened and Skosh caught a glimpse of Charlie, still and silent as a specter, waiting for him to pass before going on to the next room. Lowell led the way out of the building and across a paved assembly area toward a shed in the darkening forest at the edge of the compound.

Dusk dampened all sounds. Even the wind had stilled. Their boots crunched through thin ice atop a cinder path as they walked. Skosh saw Lowell beckon to an invisible man in a shadow with a jerk of his head and realized they had other orders concerning him that no amount of American officialdom would countermand. Gurin knew damn well Uncle Sam would deny any knowledge of his existence, just as Moscow would never have heard of Ignat.

Skosh prepared accordingly, casually turning his head in a narrow arc as he scanned the open area before the shed.

Lowell struck too early. The other man was still three yards away and could do nothing. Skosh broke his attacker's windpipe and used an upward thrusting elbow to snap his head back, then planted a front kick to the solar plexus, pushing him into his would-be assistant. They both fell, one of them dying, the other pinned beneath the body.

Skosh retrieved his H&K pistol from the dying thief's holster and considered. He had no suppressor on it and did not want to raise an alarm, but the other man was rolling out from under the body. It was time to make a decision. He ran behind the man before he could stand fully upright and broke his neck.

Sergei sauntered out of the forest at that moment, silent, with eyebrows raised. He must have seen it, thought Skosh. Of course, he saw it.

Of all the people he never wanted to see in that moment, Jade stood behind Sergei's right shoulder.

Sergei kept his voice low as he handed over the SIG Sauer and Mack's knife. And Jade.

"She is rightfully your problem."

She looked like hell, but there was no time to wonder why.

Skosh had killed two men. And now he was being given access to a specialist's weapons, not just any specialist, either. Misha was more like specialist royalty. Mack, he reminded himself. You don't have the right to call him Misha. You don't want that right. But it was the irritable, adrenaline-filled specialist attitude in himself that irked the most. He was taking orders from Sergei as though they were equals.

THIRTY-NINE

Skosh knew Mack could read what had just happened on his face as he handed him the knife. There was a speculative look, a question mark in those blue eyes. He responded with his first-ever successful blank stare. This might be the end of his career as a babysitter, but he refused to be propelled into the shitty world of the specialist.

Mack glanced briefly at Jade and gave a silent signal that directed them both to disappear. Skosh concurred. He never wanted to be near their work. But as they stepped out of the shed, the entire compound became brightly lit, as though by the flip of a single switch.

Deep shadows cast by corners of various wooden buildings no doubt contained enough firepower to save Prion, but because of his experience with Charlemagne, Skosh knew better than to place any bets on the man's survival. He heard the occasional scrape of footsteps on gravel in the still night air, then the muted sounds of two suppressors on the far side of the compound, or was that three?

He plastered himself and Jade against a wall in a narrow shadow at one side of the prison hut, feeling exposed. He still had not seen Mack since cutting him free. A body fell out of a shadowed corner of the next building over. A lessening fountain of blood sparkled under the bright light at the center.

That would be Mack's work, thought Skosh.

Jade vomited. Luckily, she hadn't eaten much and was soon able to move with him. He was deciding where it might be safer when an unsuppressed burst of rifle fire ended the relative stillness.

Skosh had seen the muzzle flash of that burst. It was forward and to their left. He pulled Jade to the right, briefly considering slipping back into the prison hut when another gunman ran from one shadow to the next on a course that threatened to put them uncomfortably close to the action.

At the first sound of a suppressed zip from what must be more firing by the team, he hit the ground, bearing Jade with him and covering her with his body.

…

Misha let the body drop and ran crouching toward the sound of the MP5s, then veered in the direction of the first burst from an AK. He found the shooter forming a sight picture on another shadow. The SIG had been returned to him without its suppressor, but once the gun battle began, stealth was no longer necessary. He fired and the shooter dropped. The other shadow ran toward him, diving into the shade on his side of the shed.

"Thanks," said Steve. He took a moment to catch his breath. "I'm counting the hired tangos to make sure we got 'em all. Michael took a bullet in his back. Not deep. Vest worked. Kind of. Said to tell you to see to the two principals. He can't. They're hiding in the big building. Kestutis and Rimas are here. They helped clear the American barrack. Mara is injured. Sergei's been ordered to back you up."

Both of his children. Both. Misha stamped it down; could feel the anger growing. Wanted to spray automatic fire into the already dead. Wanted to obliterate the still-living.

Steve spoke again. "I got the guy who shot Michael."

Misha looked at him and noticed he held his MP5 in the wrong hand. He looked at the other. It hung uselessly. Even in shadow, he caught a glint of wetness dripping from the fingers. He nodded.

He stepped sideways to peer at the main building from around the corner of this shed.

As he stepped the other way, Steve added, "Michael said to tell you he'll live. So will Mara."

It was going to be a joy to kill Prion, not an act of despair.

Misha sauntered into the tableau of aftermath in the center of the compound, where Kestutis stood swaying in the light calling Prion a fucking coward at top volume, in English.

He waited, instinctively understanding what the team needed, what the Lithuanians wanted, and what he required. As Prion and Gurin stepped out of the door and stood under the floodlights, he held his fire.

...

Jade wondered why it was so loud. Then she remembered being required to wear ear protection on the Army range. All those gun battles in the movies never show the hearing shift. The suppressed weapons did not hurt as much as the AKs, which made her ears ring even after the gunfire stopped.

Skosh helped her up, and they stood together quietly in the shadow cast by Misha's former jail.

She counted the people standing. Prion and Gurin stood before the doors of the main building, both of them holding pistols. Mack, absolutely still, faced them to their right, the muzzle of his SIG smoking in the cold air. The dissipating heat from other muzzles helped her pinpoint two members of the team still in shadow.

Kestutis faced Prion from a distance of ten yards. Rimas stood next to him. They did not have their guns raised, but Jade could see the weapons in their hands at their sides.

Kestutis began proceedings.

"Who are you working for?" he asked Prion.

"I work for myself. I told you."

"Why are you here?"

"To help Lithuania. Again, I told you that."

"But I heard you hate my country."

"Of course not. I only want what's best for it. You know Lithuania is only weakened by people like that pervert who is trying to steal my son's money."

"Are you saying we are too naive to know what is best for us?"

Prion paused and reddened under the bright lights, then blurted "Sometimes, like my ex-wife, you are too stupid to know what's right!"

Gurin held up a hand in a calming gesture.

Jade watched as Kestutis mastered his anger. The lines relaxed with his jaw. He looked younger. It was then that she saw him sway. Rimas held his left arm to steady him. As he raised the gun in his hand, she saw that the side of his jacket had stuck to him like it was wet.

"I see that it is you who are not right," said Kestutis. "You hate too much, for too little reason, and you infected me with it, and for what?"

"For patriotism, for your country, for decency!"

Jade wanted badly to complete it with '…and the American way' to highlight the hypocrisy.

Kestutis muttered 'decency' as he eyed Gurin.

The banker spoke up.

"Please understand, we mean no harm to Lithuania. Only good. Such impulses must not prevail in a strong nation. They are unpatriotic."

It was the kind of argument that appealed to Kestutis. Jade could see him mentally tasting it, but before he could speak, Sergei stepped out of a shadow to their left, dressed as the fighter he was, festooned with weapons, ammunition, and radios, face painted in camo colors, twigs in his unruly hair. With one arm he supported his wife, similarly dressed, as she limped by his side, leaving a patch of blood behind each step of her right foot. Both carried MP5s in their free hands.

"Hello, Ignat. It has been a long time," Sergei said quietly.

He said it in English, but Gurin responded to him in a long stream of Russian, emphasizing every other word. He did everything but spit deliberately, though there was plenty of the involuntary kind. He also raised his gun, pointing the muzzle toward Sergei.

Jade did not understand the words, though the sentiments were clear. Kestutis understood both. At first, she wondered who shot Gurin, there were so many candidates. In the next moment, she realized the suppressed MP5s would not have been that loud. As the man fell, so did the man who shot him, Kestutis. The lights above them picked out the spreading red stain on his jacket. Rimas knelt beside him.

Prion let go a stream of English swear words as he swung the muzzle of his gun toward the dying man.

Charlemagne's newest member fulfilled its deadly commission. Unready and in a crouch, Rimas placed a single bullet in Prion's forehead.

FORTY

Rimas heard the Challenger's wheels go up but resisted the urge to sleep while he contemplated the ring. It had been a gift from Kestutis as he lay dying and was too small for any finger but his pinkie, so he wore it there. Fighters of the past were smaller, he surmised, because nutritious food could be scarce in a forest bunker.

Kestutis apologized for trying to find and kill Antanas.

"You hid him well," he had said, as Rimas knelt beside him. "He was not in Šiauliai."

"No."

"Where?" The word caused a wince.

"Vilnius. Užupis."

The dying man nodded, then raised his hand. The ring had been on his pinkie as well.

"Take it," he said. "My father gave it to me. It is the ring of the Kestutis partisan regiment, after the second Soviet invasion. Žemaitis himself gave it to him. My father followed his example during the war and did not participate in the killings. He had judgment. He tried to pass it on to me with the ring."

Kestutis paused in an effort to breathe. Rimas sought a way to comfort him, but the dying man continued in a broken voice.

"He failed."

After another pause for tortured breath, "I was a fool ... should have known better. Learn from me. If you like or do not like ... do not follow ... or kill."

Rimas slid the ring from his teacher's finger but kept hold of the hand.

"Your father did not fail with you, Kestutis. Your judgment prevailed in the end. My brother is alive. The false American did not succeed."

Kestutis murmured with his last breath, "Because of you."

…

"What did the doctor say? How soon must you have surgery? Are you in pain? I can give you something. The op is over. You can have something for pain."

"Sergei, stop," said Mara. "I will be fine. There is no need to break the rule. I can wait until we are at altitude."

She heard the whine of the engines starting and thumps beneath them as the rest of the team stowed their gear. The pain was incredible, but she could not show Sergei. He would pitch a fit about her ever coming out on an op again. She could not bear that.

"It should have been me," he said. He fussed with her seatbelt, put a fresh bottle of water in the cup holder next to her, and patted her hand.

Five words, she thought. With five words everything she thought she knew about herself, about what she wanted, about what was wise, changed. What if it had been him?

She gasped and he looked at her with alarm. Eight words.

What if it had been both of them?

"Sergei, I think we must make a difficult decision."

His grey eyes opened wide, but he had the sense to wait for the rest before replying.

"Yelena will be four years old next month," said Mara. "When I was growing up, I always had my mother even when my father was away."

"You wish to stay home?"

"Of course not," she said with some heat. "I cannot be a housewife or whatever the term is."

"You want me to stay home with Yelena?"

She looked at him. He was prepared to do that for her. She could see it on his face, and she knew it would kill a part of him, a part that made him so dear to her. She loved every scar on his body, every joke he told, funny or not, and the way he touched her, cradled her, loved her. She could not do that to him.

"No, Sergei. What is that phrase Misha always uses when he wants someone to put up with something unpleasant?"

"Operational necessity."

"That's it. I will not like to stay home, and neither will you, but Yelena should not lose both of us at once. She is old enough now to feel it. I think one of us must stay to keep her from being orphaned during just one op."

He bowed his head over her hand, lifted it, and kissed her bloody fingers. As the airplane taxied and the others took their seats, he gazed at her. They understood each other perfectly.

"It will not be the same to be out without you to watch my back," he said. "And as you say, I will hate staying home when it is my turn. But you are correct. It is an operational necessity."

...

"What did you tell Jade about your plan, Michael?"

Misha sipped a fine whiskey and waited for his son's reply.

"I told her we would offer her in exchange for Rimas."

"And she agreed?"

"I said we would rescue her—eventually."

Misha raised an eyebrow. "I saw her reaction when I surrendered to them. I thought she would faint again. It took the idiot hiding behind her too long to think of putting a gun to her head."

"She has grown to like you. I am amazed." Michael wondered if age would soften him enough to become likable to normal people. He shifted sideways in his reclining seat to ease the pain in his back and to look at his father.

"Only as a father figure, I am sure," said Misha.

"That kiss was not fatherly."

Michael was reminded by his father's answering grin that the man had been smiling a lot lately. More than he could ever remember while growing up. He had once been able to manage a wide grin and could still smile gently—within the family. Would joyful grins ever return? How old would he have to be? Would he live long enough?

"Tell me again why I was required to surrender so ignominiously," said Misha.

"It was hardly ignominious, Papa. You took out three within minutes."

"And surrendered to only two, both of them barely competent in a fight. Why?"

"To unbalance Gurin so he would betray himself to Kestutis."

They both sipped thoughtfully. Misha splashed a bit more into his glass, raising the bottle with a questioning look. Michael shook his head.

"It did unbalance him," he insisted. "Gurin could not resist such a chance. He was beside himself with glee. We have it on tape."

"But it did not save Kestutis."

"No. That is true. Kestutis took out the sniper who hit Mara."

"Your plan worked. It also made a specialist of Rimas."

"How did you know, Papa, that he would fit us so well?"

"Because I knew Kestutis. He had judgment when he was younger."

"It must have deserted him."

Misha grimaced into his glass. "There was a time when he better resisted his prejudices. It is difficult to know friends from enemies and to separate patriotism from fanaticism. In the end, he remembered verification is not optional."

Michael considered asking for more in his glass but knew he was losing the battle against sleep, the sleep that would help ease the pain, though he would dream about it as he always did when injured. His father's next words propped his eyes open, all thoughts of sleep banished.

"I will not come out with you next time, Michael."

"You will retire? Can you bear it?"

Misha shrugged. "I mean to try."

"Alex will be happy."

"She will be very happy. So will the ghosts of my youth. Kestutis is the last whose fate I ever wish to know about. I prefer to allow the others to live on in my memory as they were when I knew them." He finished his whiskey. "I think I will help Tobias move the cattle up to the summer pastures this year."

Michael searched his father's face, peered into those impossibly prescient blue eyes, and saw the same man he had always known. There was no sign of sickness or softening. He signaled for a splash more whiskey in both their glasses. Misha obliged.

"We have taken more damage than usual, Papa. I hope I will fill the gap you leave, but I think it is a good thing," he said, smiling wryly, "to make such a decision when you know you are not past it."

Misha smiled. "Oh, you may always call upon me when you need a dangle. I have discovered I have a particular talent for playing the bait."

FORTY-ONE

They sat in embarrassed silence. Skosh reminded himself he was only surmising Jade's mood. He knew why he was mortified and reviewed why he thought she shared the feeling. During takeoff, he had twice caught her glancing at him, then hurriedly looking away. Of course, he was doing the same, avoiding eye contact, glancing surreptitiously, trying not to be caught at it.

The conclusion that she was embarrassed was also supported by her blushes each time he caught her turning away.

But the definitive proof had come from Mack.

Uwe, not Claire, was flying them back to the U.S. in the Lear Jet. Claire would fly the Challenger, Mack said, to be home with her injured husband, Steve.

Skosh had argued.

"Look, we can fly commercial. I don't know how you intend to bill Uncle Sam for these flights, but our money people will not be thrilled that we got to ride in style—both ways, even. They'll take it out of my fucking hide, or rather, my paycheck."

Mack gave him the blue glare Skosh had learned usually meant more than 'you are an imbecile cheapskate,' but he wasn't sure about the rest. It took a few extra moments before Mack coughed up a minimal assurance and a devastating counter-argument to taking an airline flight. Devastating because it demolished his protest and informed him about the last thing he had ever wanted to know.

"We will not charge for it," said Mack. "Jade should not fly on a commercial airline."

That was it. A complete explanation in the most minimalist expression the bastard could give it. Each successive thought brought Skosh lower.

They were flying courtesy of the team because of Jade.

'Jade should not' did not mean she was somehow special, but that the issue involved security—her security. It was at issue because she could be connected with a member of Charlemagne. The newest member.

The bastards. When had they arranged it? While they were ransacking the place for documents and other intelligence. While he had been busy on the phone—to the resident, to Kestutis's ministry, to police, to the doctor on standby. There were too many sleeping quarters in the compound, with plenty of beds.

"He's too new," Skosh had said, trying to mask the desperation he felt. "Nobody even knows about him; no one will connect them yet."

Mack answered with a glare.

"At least …" Skosh faltered, then resumed. "At least keep the surveillance unobtrusive so she won't notice."

He was not sure whether Mack's slight head tilt meant yes or no.

…

The last person Jade knew anything about at this moment was herself. Oh, she knew her history and her favorite color, her best outfit and most comfortable shoes. But aside from a steadfast love for her cat, Sekmet, her feelings gurgled and bounced in random patterns between mind and heart.

She could not look at Skosh, no matter how much she wanted to. He would see her blush. He would know with that mysterious male sixth sense about the sex she'd had but not with him.

Rimas had been hasty and vehement, pouring all his emotions into the act, emotions that he must have stuffed down a black hole until they erupted into and around and through her body. She had seen his cool, unemotional gaze when he shot Prion. That the two could be the same man unsettled her. She decided she preferred the emotional Rimas to his killing alter-ego.

And what about Mack? Had he meant that kiss? Surely not. He was making a point that had nothing to do with her. But did his surrender at the safehouse mean he was willing to die for her after all? She remembered how safe she had felt with him, despite the threats. Then she watched him kill three men.

So what did she feel? Respect, certainly, and a kind of affection that she had never before experienced for such a strange being. She caught herself on the last thought. She did know this feeling. It resembled her attachment to her own carnivorous hunter, Sekmet.

Her heart sank beneath her feet as she contemplated Skosh. A heart this low must be in love, she thought, but how is that possible? Infatuated, definitely, but love? He would not look at her. He must be angry. Mack said there was no hope. Why? Because he is honorable. What the hell did that mean?

At least she knew her mind regarding Skosh. She wanted him with every molecule of her being but strongly suspected Mack was right. Maybe on another planet he could be wrong, or in a fourth dimension, a parallel universe where Rimas had not happened and where being honorable didn't mean it had to be impossible.

What the hell did Mack mean?

Skosh sat across the little table from her. Two hours into the flight, after days of complete exhaustion, neither of them had even tried to sleep. She caught his eye.

"You meant that last kiss, Skosh."

He raised his eyebrows, dumbfounded.

"Yes, I did."

At least he admitted it.

"So did I," she said.

He paused, then said, "I know."

"So what did Mack mean when he told me it would be impossible because you are honorable?"

She had to know both what it meant and whether it was true. No matter how much it might hurt.

He sighed, frowning. "It's complicated."

"Try me."

"I have power in the organization. I can't form a… a relationship with anybody I could conceivably hurt. I can't because it's vicious and because it was done to me. That's what Mack meant. But hey, chances are pretty good I'll be unemployed shortly and then I can have a relationship with anybody who'll have me. Anybody free, that is, which you are not."

"I am free, Skosh, and surely that won't happen. Mack said he would do what he could. He's omnipotent. And you can't affect my job. You're not in my chain of command."

He snorted. "There you go with that military shit again. I will always be in your chain, as you call it, every time I—we—go out on an op because you will go with me. You'll be requested to assist me, or to assist my replacement, from now on."

It was her turn to snort. "Rimas will move on as the memory fades. I'll just say no when the personnel people call. You can get somebody else to go with you. That's all. Find another assistant."

Preferably male, she thought.

Skosh leaned forward, locking eyes with her as he said in a low growl, "Jade, you saw almost every member of the team come out of this op injured or at least badly bruised. It was a light outcome for them, given the odds. There has been a time in their history when the only reason one of them wasn't considered badly injured after an op was because he was dead."

His words made her shiver, but she stiffened herself.

"I'm sorry for that, but I am hardly qualified to change it. I'd be more of a liability than an assistant. It was my fault Mack was captured."

Skosh froze with his mouth open, shook himself, and replied with some heat.

"Jade, that was part of Charlie's plan."

"It was?"

"Yes."

He watched her face turn pale as she took in this revelation.

"His father?"

"Can I ask what you thought you were going to do with his weapons in that pillowcase? Just curious. I think everybody is curious."

"I was going to find where they took him, sneak in and rescue him, then give him his gun so he could defend himself. I figured I owed him. He rescued me from Kestutis."

"And the knife? The one you pulled out of a dead guy?"

"I would need something to cut the zip ties he was tied with."

Skosh could not fully comprehend how such a woman had come into his orbit. He wanted her to never change. He wanted the universe to stand still. But his duty required that he enlighten her, just a little.

"You need to understand a lot of things, Jade, but let's start with what's immediate. Anything you thought you knew about relationships and obligations doesn't work here. You and I are in a kind of triangle now, and the third member is a working specialist."

He took a deep breath to support the next thing he had to say.

"I know you like Rimas."

She opened her mouth to protest but closed it again because it was true. She wanted to say, 'Not more than I like you,' but what good would that do?

Skosh continued softly, "You can't tell me you'll say no when he could be dead the next day. You're not that cold-blooded, or I am much mistaken about you. It is part of what attracts us both to you."

The effort it had taken him to admit this to her and to himself made him sit back and shake his head before finishing the thought with a sad smile.

"Neither of us—none of us—is free anymore."

EPILOGUE

This is when they'll fire me, thought Skosh. He sat at a table before a raised dais. On the dais, behind another table, sat three men: his boss's boss, Henry, his boss, Bill (not his real name), and a colleague from another office. He tried to remember Seeker's real name.

Bill began proceedings.

"We are here, Skosh, to give you the results of our investigation into the data breach of your section's library computer system last month while you were out of the office conducting an operation in ..." He looked down at the document before him, turned the page, turned it back, found the name and said, "Lith-oo-ain-ee-a."

It surprised Skosh that even after five years in his position, Bill was still unfamiliar with the geography his subordinates experienced daily. Bill had been a first-rate field officer and Middle East expert. Skosh could see he longed to go back there.

He could identify. It had broken his heart to leave Asian operations to someone else and learn two more languages, recently adding French as required by edict of Mack. But he had done it and also learned enough about his subordinates' work to hold an occasional intelligent conversation with them.

Bill's boss, Henry, piped in with, "I see that you took seriously my admonition about information security, Skosh. I commend you for that." He looked to Bill to continue.

"We interviewed Penelope Prendergast, the chief librarian," said Bill, "who accompanied you on the op, her assistant Dennis Watson, and Candace Seston, who ran administration quality control."

Skosh hoped he did not betray how startled he was to hear Candace named. He found the past tense verb 'ran' also concerning.

Bill chewed his pen a moment before continuing. "We also conducted extensive forensic examinations by qualified computer experts to try to pinpoint the source of the intrusion."

Henry interrupted again at this point.

"Watson and Prendergast explained the system you devised to both fulfill the terms of that unfortunate agreement with the operatives who had the commission and maintain info security. Again, I commend you."

Was Seeker looking just a little sour? Both sour and superior, Skosh decided as the man leaned back in his chair and threw his eyes toward Bill.

"Yes, well," said his boss, "aside from that, we do have an issue to resolve regarding your conduct in this."

"My conduct?"

"Yes. But first, let me give you the findings of the forensic computer examiner. It seems the breach came through Ms. Seston's computer. She denies it entirely and denies knowing your password, but she did have a program installed on her machine that could run through various combinations and eventually break in. We believe this is what happened."

Seeker leaned over and whispered something.

"I'm getting to that," Bill said irritably. He looked back at Skosh. "In the course of this extended investigation, we discovered that you had been having an affair with Ms. Seston...."

"Once," interrupted Skosh. "We had sex, not an affair. Once."

"Let me finish. It was highly unprofessional of you...."

"Me?"

"Yes, you. We believe that she was motivated to break into the system as an act of revenge for her broken heart. She inserted an unfortunate clause in the agreement with your operatives and then caused a breach in security in an effort to blame you. Thus, you are not free of all culpability in this incident."

"I am junior to her."

Seeker gave him a pitying look. "Come, come, Skosh. You're the man in the relationship. The man is always the pursuer. The poor woman had no choice but to fall in with your proposition."

"There was no relationship. The poor woman made the proposition. She was the senior party to a not even one-hour stand."

Skosh uttered this defense through clenched teeth.

"Nonetheless," said Bill, "you are to be verbally counseled. It will not be part of your record unless you are found to be involved in any more incidents of the same nature. You are directed to have no further contact with Ms. Seston. She has been similarly directed. I expect you to respect her situation and cease all communication."

"Her situation?"

"Her security clearance has been downgraded and as a result, she was relocated to a less sensitive division in another state. Any more questions?"

"No."

"Do you understand the conclusions and instructions of this tribunal?"

"Yes."

"Will you initiate an appeal against any or all of our findings?"

Skosh's first instinct was to say, 'fuck yeah,' but he remembered that twenty minutes before, he had assumed he'd be dismissed and sanctioned—the final kind of sanction.

"No. I will not appeal."

Bill smiled. "Then you are hereby verbally counseled not to conduct sexual relationships with any coworkers who may perceive a power imbalance between you."

Seeker smirked.

Skosh could not help his next words. "How about Seeker here? He's my equal and he's male, or so he says. Can I have sex with him?"

Seeker's glare suggested he should eat shit and die.

Bill scowled, rolled his eyes, gathered his papers, then filed out with the other two.

Skosh sat contemplating the shaky nature of his status quo. To all appearances, he'd had a serendipitous escape. He had prepared himself for ultimate disaster and was ready to die when Mack pulled his hand away as it held the knife point at his belly.

Serendipity in the person of Mack now owned his very life.

The End

How will the Skosh-Jade-Rimas triangle affect the survivability of the team, and who will be responsible for the damage? Look for the next Charlemagne File, *Goat Rope*, at your favorite bookstore.

Join the Charlemagne Files newsletter for more stories and information about the series, its world of covert operations, and the lives of the characters on the team. Sign up here: https://www.charlemagnefiles.com/contact

If you enjoyed this book, please consider leaving a short review at your favorite bookstore.

CHARLEMAGNE AND THE SECTION

The fictional world of The Section follows a few conventions. It may help the first-time reader of The Charlemagne Files to know some of these.

Who/what/ where is The Section?

The Section is a department of an intelligence agency of the United States. Its employees are civil servants. It includes support staff members who provide identity documents, financial controls, and physical and document security. The offices are near the East Coast, maybe Virginia.

The operational agents are called babysitters. They arrange on-site logistical support for freelance specialists during operations. Most operations are not conducted within the United States, with some exceptions.

Babysitters themselves do not carry identity documents in their names during an operation and never carry any official identification from their organization. Their purpose is to allow the organization to deny any association with them or their mission.

Nicknames

Babysitters in The Section receive nicknames from their coworkers when they join the office. These names are often undesirable and used mercilessly among the members of the office. It is part of the team-building process in a stressful occupation.

Coins

Challenge coins are traditionally stamped with symbols or mottos that designate the intelligence unit of their owners. The tradition is that when members of the unit are present at the bar and one produces his coin, all must produce theirs. Anyone failing to show their coin is responsible for the bar tab. If all produce their coins, then the challenger who first produced his or her coin is responsible for the tab.

File designations

The highest classification of information is Top Secret. Beyond Top Secret, more sensitive information is strictly controlled in a number of ways including designation as Sensitive Compartmented Information (SCI). This requires an additional clearance and often a named clearance based on Need-To-Know.

In The Section, files on specialists or specialist teams receive a one-word code name, printed across the file and restricted to very few people. When a solo or specialist team is employed on an operation, another designator word will refer to the operation and will be used for funding, reports, etc.

The Section's file name for Charlemagne is WEDGE. Thus CETUS WEDGE (second book of the Charlemagne Files) means an operation dubbed CETUS using the team called WEDGE.

Specialist

A team or solo operative used by Western governments for black operations conducted without fingerprints in high-risk situations expected to involve death.

GLOSSARY OF NAMES

Linda and David Bertram - widow and son of the late mole, Richard Bertram (*Brevet Wedge* and *Vory*); deceased.

Viktor Borodinov - alias John Earnest, alias Paul Crutchfield, CFO of Brighton Associates, SVR agent.

Frank Cardova - long-time babysitter of Charlemagne; later, head of The Section; retired by the time of *Vory*; real name is Leo Vilseck; Section nickname is Buddy.

Antanas Dockus (Dots-kūs) - brother of Rimantas.

Rimantas Dockus (Dots-kūs) - called Rimas, protégé of Kestutis.

Claire Donovan - deputy chief pilot employed by Charlemagne, married to Steve Donovan.

Steve Donovan - member of Charlemagne; martial artist; former fighter pilot; abandoned real name was Daniel Martin Kessler..

The Frenchman - deceased marksman and technical expert of Charlemagne; real name is Louis; last name is unknown.

Justin Goodwin - FBI special agent and IT specialist; no aliases.

Sally Kessler - ex-wife of Steve Donovan; deceased.

Danny Kessler - son of Steve Donovan.

Kestutis - last name unknown. Son and grandson of anti-Soviet Lithuanian forest-based partisans, now a counter-intelligence officer in the Lithuanian security service, appointed as liaison to Skosh.

Mack - so dubbed by Western babysitters because he uses a knife at times; leader and decision maker of Charlemagne; called Misha by other members of his team; probable real name is Michael; last name is unknown.

Michael - Misha's son. Game name Charlie.

Misha - long-time founder and leader of Charlemagne. Called Mack by non-team members.

John Nakamura - official game name. Usually called by his Section nickname, Skosh; successor to Frank Cardova.

Sergei Pavlenko - former KGB agent, now the gadget and explosives expert of Charlemagne. Married to Mara.

Mara Sobieski Pavlenko - computer expert and marksman of Charlemagne. Daughter of Vasily Sobieski, the team's deceased explosives expert. Biological daughter of Misha, half-sister of Michael, married to Sergei Pavlenko.

Earl Prion - an American millionaire whose ex-wife was a Lithuanian.

Skosh - The Section nickname for John Nakamura, a game name. Skosh's real name is undisclosed. Charlemagne's American babysitter.

Alexandra Sobieski - widow of Vasily Sobieski and daughter of former Charlemagne babysitter and head of The Section Fred Dolnikov; no aliases; now married to Mack.

Vasily Sobieski - deceased explosives expert and martial artist whose father was a noted solo specialist; no aliases.

Charlie Taylor - marksman; son of Mack; probable real name is Michael; last name unknown.

Jay Turner - FBI counterintelligence agent with a private agenda;
no aliases.

Maryann Vilseck - wife of Leo Vilseck, aka Frank Cardova.

Theresa Vilseck - daughter of Leo Vilseck.

Karl Weltung - Prion's banker.

Jade Wilmerton - game name of Penelope Prendergast, Chief Administrator of The Section Vault.